Keywords and Concepts
Hindustani Classical Music

Keywords
and Concepts
Hindustani
Classical
Music

Ashok Da. Ranade

NEW DELHI
PROMILLA & CO., PUBLISHERS

First published 1990 in India by Promilla and Co.,
Publishers, 'Sonali,' C-127, Sarvodaya Enclave, New Delhi 110 017

ISBN 81 85002 12 6

Ranade, Ashok D. (Ashok Damodar), 1937-
    Keywords and concepts : Hindustani classical music /
Ashok Da. Ranade. — New Delhi : Promilla, 1990.

    xii, 160 p. : ill. ; 23 cm.
    Biblography: p. [128]-132.
    Includes index.
    ISBN 81 85002 12 6

    1. Music, Hindustani—Dictionaries. I. Title.

Illustrations : V. N. O'key

Printed in India by Gayatri Offset Press, NOIDA, Ghaziabad
Typeset and Processed by Akshar Pratiroop Pvt. Ltd., Bombay

For Meena and Arun Naik

Preface

I learnt Hindustani vocal classical music in the well-known *guru-shishya* tradition. Hence I never asked questions but absorbed innumerable insights which gradually fell into a well-knit pattern during a period of about twenty years. In a performance-oriented tradition this was but natural.

The training convinced me that theory and practice of music cohere better when performers themselves theorize. It soon became clear that the so-called 'illiterate' performers have been theorizing all through the centuries, both verbally and non-verbally! They theorized and performed almost simultaneously. In the final analysis, relationship of all performing arts to other life ensured that a majority of theorizations became verbalized to form a scholastic tradition.

Thus was created a majestic edifice of concepts and terms that echoes the life of music to a great extent. To understand these is to map the musical heavens!

To bring together themes, concepts and terms led inevitably to the *Amarkosha*-format. The original plan envisaged including sections on music education and scholarship, folk and primitive music, popular music and music and culture.

I hope to do so in the near future.

Ashok Da. Ranade

Bombay,
Dasara, 10 October 1989

The use

The table of contents lists the major sections and headings that have a separate entry.

The detailed index indicates terms that occur in the text and also those which enjoy an independent entry.

It would be helpful to read introductions to each of the sections along with the specific entry one is looking up.

Contemporary music is the take-off point, and the historical, grammatical-technical aspects are kept to the minimum.

The pronunciation-key devised is deliberately simplified for laymen who, one hopes, would like to use the book. The key is given in the end, as its use is restricted to the index.

Abbreviations and symbols:

1. *Source Language*
   Arabic   A
   Hindi   H
   Persian   P
   Sanskrit   S

2. *Parts of Speech*
   Adjective   adj
   Adverb   adv
   Noun   (not mentioned)
   Verb   v

3. *Etymology is indicated by < sign along with the parent language and/or part of speech.*

4. *indicates main entry elsewhere.*

Contents

List of Illustrations

1. Music making

Music is a performing art, and hence music-making is the life force of all music-related activities. Learning, practising, studying, appreciating or even criticizing music, needs a base in music-making.

Music is made in many ways, under various circumstances and by different people. It has many modes of coming into being. Artistes, accompanists, the audience and particularly the knowledgeable listeners, have roles to play when music is created. The entire endeavour is governed by unwritten but definite norms. Thus music does make partners of us all!

Music begins, flourishes, ends, it lingers behind. Some take naturally to the flow of music; some allow it to pass by.

Fortunately, very few suffer the ignominy of remaining untouched by the Ganga of music!

For those who wish to be blessed by the touch of music, it helps to know music and have a feel of its magic. This effort is for those who seek to know about music.

1.1 *Occasion*
Sometimes music is in itself a sufficient provocation to make music! It is like the Everest, to be scaled because it is there! However, music is often made in order to mark an occasion, fittingly and properly. The nature of the occasion determines the motivation, environment, repertoire and the format. The presentation accordingly undergoes changes; hence the need to understand the character of the occasion for which music is made.

1.1.1 *Baithak* (H *baithana* = to sit)
Except in folk or tribal music, a concert of music is described as *baithak.* Etymological connections hint at the modalities adopted by artistes and listeners who enjoy music during performances. Usually

both are seated on mattresses etc. laid on the floor. This is in obvious contrast to the modern use of chairs for the listeners and raised platforms for the artistes.

Baithak can also mean a drawing room, depending on the nature of the occasion. A patron, at his own sweet will and initiative, invites select persons to listen to an established or an 'up and coming' artiste. Till at least the beginning of the twentieth century, *baithaks* were not ticketed. In all probability, one major patron paid or rewarded the artiste. However, to receive contributions from friends as a support was not ruled out. Even today the *baithak* has not gone out of vogue.

As an institution, *baithak* is traceable to *goshthi* (S. assembly). By 200 A.D., a complete *goshthi*-culture was prevalent. There were various kinds of *goshthi*s in which an assembly could enjoy *vina* (lute), *vadya* (instrumental music), *geet* (singing) etc. To convene a *goshthi* was a prerogative of a *nagaraka*, an accomplished urbanite (*nagar* means a city). A person who conducted *goshthi*s decorously was known as a *goshthi-pati* (leader of the assembly). Alternatively the *goshthi*s could be convened at the initiative of a *ganika* (meaning a courtesan) well versed in the sixty-four arts identified by works on ancient Indian culture.

The idiom of the language confirms the strong musical association of the verb *baithana* 'to sit'. Musicians frequently employ expressions such as *aaj baithenge* etc. to indicate arrangement of a music performance.

It may be noted that *baithak* also refers to the sitting postures of performers, certain postures being more conducive to music- making than certain others. However, this discussion takes us to another area, that of actual performing activity itself.

1.1.2 *Barasi* (anniversary H < S *varsha* = year)
The death anniversary of a musician or a saint may be observed through a music performance. The main intention is to honour or respect the memory of the person.

*Barasi*s of Muslim saints, or *sufi*s, *pir*s (*pir* = *guru*, preceptor) inspire longer festivals known as *Urs* in which music forms an important component.

1.1.3 *Davat* (A)
A resident musician may host a ceremonial dinner in honour of a visiting musician. Recognized musicians are invited to attend the per-

formance given by the visiting artiste on the occasion.

Basically, *davat* (invitation) is useful as it introduces the visiting musician to the local celebrities who then can spread his name in the right quarters.

1.1.4 *Hazri* (A)

Means presence before the respected. Performers present themselves in a temple or in a court to perform, and describe the act as *hazri dena*, meaning 'to give a performance out of respect'. This surely is a rather modest way of characterizing one's own effort. The Sanskrit equivalent for the practice is *seva* (meaning to serve, wait or attend upon, honour, worship, obey). It is interesting to note that according to the Hindu religious tradition, at least two from the nine major modalities of devotion are music-related. They are *shravan* (listening to God's name and his praises) and *keertana* (singing God's praises).

On visiting a temple, musicians may offer performances. They may also be appointed to offer performances at certain temples regularly. Both types of performances are known as *hazri*.

1.1.5 *Karyakrama* (S *karya* = work, affair, business + *krama* = sequence)

It connotes a single and independent presentation of almost any kind. The term came into circulation as a music-related linguistic usage sometime during the twentieth century. It symbolizes the more formalized nature of music-making as well as the more systematized organization of the musical event. It retains its validity irrespective of the modality, the purpose, the audience and the organizing agency involved, provided the performances form a complete unit.

1.1.6 *Mehfil* (A)

Essentially synonymous with *baithak*, *mehfil* is a place where a music or dance-performance is in progress. It is significant that the *sufis* (Muslim mystics) describe the world as a *mehfil*. The *sufis* virtually acted as a bridge between Hindu and Islamic mysticism and thus earned a place for themselves in India in the eleventh century. It needs to be stressed that Hindustani music is rich in *sufi* associations and many of its characteristic features become intelligible if the *sufi* way of life is borne in mind. The term *mehfil* is important in this light. It is significant that Shakespeare compared the world to a stage: the *sufis* preferred a musical model to depict it!

1.1.7 *Mela* (H < S *melaka* = that which brings together)
Music-making in a festival celebrated to honour a Hindu deity, saint
etc., is popularly known as a *mela*.

Some of the *mela*s have been known for their long tradition: they at-
tract musicians, music-lovers and devotees alike. Invitation to par-
ticipate in a *mela* is usually considered to be an honour. Participants
also believe that to give a good account of oneself in a *mela* is to ensure lasting fame along with prosperity.

Usually *mela*s become institutions and develop their own lore and
customs. Some conventions followed in *mela*s may appear musical od-
dities, but being a part of the overall tradition they have enjoyed
reverent conformity. For example, Harvallabh *mela* of Shikarpur en-
couraged simultaneous rhythm accompaniment of more than four
tabla players for a single vocalist!

1.1.8 *Parishad* (S assembly)
Today *parishad* is understood as an attempt to bring together a
variety of performers to present them successively in engagements of
short durations. It is a step towards secularizing and 'decourting' art
music to make it available to the public at a fixed price. The
phenomenon is symptomatic of the democratization processes that
struck roots in India in the nineteenth century.

Prominent features of a *parishad* are:
1. Admission is by sale of tickets or by issue of special invitations.
2. Performers from various parts of the country are invited to perform according to a predetermined schedule.
3. As a rule, performers' fees are paid in cash though they may also
   be awarded honorary titles etc.
4. Individual artistes are allowed time-slots of varied durations
   which are usually shorter than full-length concerts.
5. *Parishad*s may run over many days and nights. To hold all-night
   performances on the last day is also a practice followed frequently.
6. Due to *parishad*s, different kinds of artistes are heard and music
   becomes generally accessible. To attend *parishad*s is also considered prestigious. However, it cannot be denied that the
   heterogeneity of audiences, unevenness of presentations and the
   distancing of the audience from the artistes often reduce
   *parishad*s to occasions of festivity, levity — music being an excuse!

It is significant that of late, *parishad*s are attracting smaller audiences and many serious listeners prefer 'private' concerts. Even though it is uncharitable to characterize *parishad*s as mere shows, it may be said that they fail to mirror the total wealth of Hindustani music.

Examined historically it could be said that *parishad*s in modern times have been inspired by the models set by the two great Vishnus, Vishnu Narayan Bhatkhande (1860-1936) and Vishnu Digambar Paluskar (1872-1931). They established the vogue of the *parishad*s during the years 1916-1930. The efforts of these two pioneers were shot with idealistic fervour. During the first All India Music Conference organized by Bhatkhande at Baroda (1916) under the patronage of the then Maharaj of Baroda, fourteen aims of the programme were listed:

1   To take steps to protect and uplift Indian music on national lines.
2   To reduce it to a regular system such as could be easily taught to and learnt by educated men and women.
3   To provide a fairly workable uniform system of *raga*s and *tala*s, (with special reference to the Northern system of music).
4   To effect if possible such a happy fusion of the Northern and Southern systems of music as would enrich both.
5   To provide a uniform system of notation for the whole country.
6   To arrange new *raga* productions on scientific and systematic lines.
7   To consider and take further steps towards the improvement of our musical instruments under the light of our knowledge of modern science, all the while taking care to preserve our cultural identity.
8   To take steps to correct and preserve the great masterpieces of the art of music in the possession of great artistes.
9   To collect in a central library all available literature (ancient and modern) on the subject of Indian music and if necessary to publish it and render it available to students of music.
10   To examine and fix the microtones or *sruti*s of Indian music with the help of scientific instruments and high class recognized artistes to distribute them among the *raga*s.
11   To start an Indian 'Men of Music' series.
12   To conduct a monthly journal of music on up-to-date lines.
13   To raise a permanent fund for carrying on the above mentioned objectives.
14   To establish a National Academy of Music in a central place where top-class instruction in music could be given on up-to-date

lines by eminent scholars and artistes in music.

Presented at length and in the language used by Pt. Bhatkhande, the nationalist sentiment and the desire to prove the high status of Indian music could hardly be missed.

The other distinguished pioneer, Pandit Paluskar, also organised *parishad*s. Their important features were:

1   In most of the *parishad*s an exhibition of musical instruments was arranged.
2   Discussions were held on non-Indian musical features such as harmony.
3   A piano-concert was scheduled in the 1921 conference.

During the years 1916-30, about twelve conferences were inspired by the direct efforts of the two Vishnus. Since then, music *parishad*s have become a regular feature of urban life. However, the original formulae have lost their drawing power, their idealism having disappeared. Many new variations have been tried out. For example, artistes of the same *gharana*, or those who could be conveniently labelled amateur, promising etc. are brought together, to hold a *parishad*.

Parishad is also called a *sammelan, samaj,* conference etc.

1.1.9 *Utsava* (S *ut* + *sav* = intense offering)
Utsava today means a festival. Traditional daily life in India allows three types of occurrences for religion and the performing arts to come together. The three are, *vrata,* meaning ritualistic observance, *parva,* or days on which particular astronomical combinations take place, and *utsava,* meaning festival. The *utsava* is important because it features the coming together of religious as well as secular tendencies and manifestations.

Some festivals seem to favour music and other performing arts. Two good examples are *Vasant panchami* and *holi.*

Celebrated on the fifth day of the *Magh shuddha* according to the Hindu calender, *Vasant panchami* ceremonially welcomes the advent of spring. Also known as worship of Saraswati (the goddess of learning), or alternatively as propitiation of Vishnu and his consort Laxmi (the goddess of wealth). Wearing yellow garments and performing music and dance form an integral part of the *utsava.* According to some authorities, the *utsava* is associated with Madan, the god of love, and Rati, his consort.

When compared to *holi* festivities, *Vasant panchami* may appear to be a rather staid affair! *Holi* falls on the full moon day of *Phalgun* and the celebrations include throwing of coloured powder or coloured water at each other, and performing music and dance. In all manifestations the erotic comes to the fore and in the rural areas even obscenity is accorded a right to surface!

These and such other *utsava*s were highly favoured by rulers of the erstwhile princely states and by members of the aristocratic families. Musicians enjoyed generous patronage during the celebrations.

Some examples would bring out the spirit of *utsava* as a phenomenon.

Rajah Tukoji Holkar (III) of Indore was a great lover of the performing arts. We are told that till 1920-22 he used to celebrate *holi* by arranging performances at three places. The one in the open spaces allowed entry to all, the second in the enclosed space was open to a select few and the third in his drawing room was only for intimate invitees. For their performing excellence, artistes were paid in silver coins heaped in a fair-sized *thali*!

The other example is from a biography of Ustad Mustaq Hussain Khan (1878-1964) of the Sahaswan *gharana*. We are told:

> It was traditional with the court of Rampur to celebrate the advent of *sawan* or the rainy season. The people of the town foregathered in mango groves. Some relaxed in hammocks hanging from the branches of trees, some quaffed thirst-quenching *sherbet*s listening to lilting melodies of the season, such as *kajri*, *jhoola* and *sawan*... Famous musicians gathered in the gardens and parks of the Nawab's palace and there were veritable feasts of *malhar*s and *kajri*s.*

Another interesting *utsava* was the one celebrated by the Benaras-based royal houses and *nawab*s. Held on Tuesday (*Mangalwar* of *Chaitra*), budwa mangal as the *utsava* was called, saw the waters of the river Ganga adorned by rows of houseboats with the king's boat at the centre flanked by those of his courtiers etc. An awning was erected on the decks and colourful chandeliers illuminated the scene. Accomplished courtesans such as Badi Maina, Chhoti Maina, Rajeshwari Shivakunwar and Badi Moti performed. Benaras courtesans sang to the accompaniment of *sitar*, *tanpura* etc., thus laying claim to sohpisticated music performance.

After the 1890s, new *utsava*s with political motivation and

(*Kshitish Roy, Sangeet Natak Akademi, New Delhi, 1964, pp 21-22)

nationalist promptings flourished and music had a place in their programme-schedules. The *Ganesh utsava* in Maharashtra and the *Durgapooja utsava* in Bengal are good examples.

1.2 Format

Format is an arrangement accepted for a particular purpose. It is also related to the way in which various members of the performing-set are distributed.

Elite or classical music in contemporary India has no choral or orchestral format. Ancient and medieval music-making, however, presented a different picture. Nowadays, performance in groups is a phenomenon confined largely to folk, primitive or popular music. In the final analysis, the format and the musical content determine each other's role: an internal logic seems to condition their relationship.

Who sits/stands where and does what?

In art-music, all performers are seated. The chief performer occupies the central position, drone accompanists are normally at the back and on both sides, rhythm accompanist operates from the right and the melodic support comes from the left in a conventional distribution of the performing-set. Examined visually the arrangement appears to guide the audience to focus its attention and thus helps better reception of the musical stimuli.

1.2.1 *Ekala* (S alone, singly)

An arrangement of the performing set in which one artiste performs with or without accompaniment. The format is employed both in rhythm-oriented and melody-oriented music.

Hindustani music-making finds the format conducive on two accounts:

1   Improvisatory procedures are inherent and important: the format proves to be the most natural way of making music. An artiste performing *ekala* is unfettered and remains in full command of the process. In case of a performer who concentrates on the tonal dimension, the accompanist operating in the rhythmic channel follows the former closely and vice versa.

2   Hindustani music lays greater store by succession and sequence rather than by simultaneity and syncopation. One note or beat at a time and one musical unit after the other, constitutes the general controlling principle. Elaboration, patterning and other musical strategies are explored in the *ekala* format.

1.2.2 *Jugalbandi* (S *yugal* = pair + A *bandi* = to bind)
While *ekala* (solo) is the reigning format in Hindustani music-making, no dynamic music culture can be expected to adhere obstinately to a single format. Variations in formats have therefore been effected through the ages. One such change in format is known as *jugalbandi*.

A co-ordinated music-making by a pair of main artistes, either in vocal or instrumental mode, with or without accompaniment, is known as *jugalbandi*. To perform in pairs has been customary. In fact musicological evidence suggests that some musical forms received their special identity *because* they were presented by a pair of chief performers.

It is usual to find two disciples of the same guru perform in the *jugalbandi* format, obviously because they find it easier to co-ordinate. Examining the contents of Hindustani music one realizes that all *raga*-music is concretized through sequences, grammatically correct and aesthetically relevant. It therefore becomes necessary that successive phrasings of the two chief participants in a *jugalbandi* result into a coherent, total pattern. Two individual insights creating a single concentrated vision is in itself a joy! In addition, *jugalbandi* gives the pleasure of variety in tonal colour in which Hindustani music is comparatively deficient.

A standardized *jugalbandi* combination is a pair of vocalists/instrumentalists accompanied by one rhythm-player. A variation might include two rhythm-accompanists inviting a description 'double *jugalbandi*'! Other pairings in the format may combine *sitar* and *sarod*, *shehnai* and violin, violin and *bansuri*, *tabla* and *pakhawaj*.

It is necessary to remember that in *jugalbandi* the basic composition such as *bandish*, *gat* etc. is presented jointly and without pronounced segmentation. Duet format may include division of the composition itself.

1.3 Performers
Hindustani musical literature employs a number of terms to denote performers. Some of the terms give us an inkling into their specialization, versatility etc. References are also made to the artistic excellence or mediocrity of the performers. There are some terms that range beyond music and refer discreetly to their social status.

The terms form a meaningful cluster. When properly appreciated, they provide an insight into the complex and sophisticated distinctions that exist among musicians.

Strictly speaking, the audience can hardly be considered to be in the performing category. However the contribution made and expected of an audience in an art-music situation in India is immeasurable, being qualitative in nature. By nods, claps, evocative utterances, occasional comments, extempore remarks etc., the audience holds a culturally-conditioned and subtly controlled dialogue with the performer through the entire performance. Anybody who merely listens to Hindustani music can hardly be considered its accredited audience! The real audience too has to 'perform' to earn that honour! About this, we shall discuss later.

1.3.1 *Atai* (A)

Atai is a person who learns quickly without anybody's help. The term has acquired more specific but contradictory musicological meanings. According to one tradition the term refers to a performer not well-versed in theory. On the other hand a performer-patron Ibrahim Adil Shah (II) (1580-1626) described *atai* as a musician of the highest order.

1.3.2 *Bajvaiyya* (H *bajana* = to play + suffix *ya baja* S *vadya* = an instrument)

It denotes a maker of instrumental music either as a soloist or an accompanist.

1.3.3 *Buzurg* (P old, advanced in age)

Connotes a performer who has long passed his prime but whose past achievements are still recognized by the musician community in general. With less frequency the term is also used to denote a connoisseur respected for his deep knowledge. *Buzurg* performers as well as listeners enjoy certain privileges.

1.3.4 *Choumukha* (H S *chatur* = four + *mukha* = mouth)

The term is a tribute to the versatility of certain art-musicians. A male singer who can render proficiently four major forms in vocal music namely, *khayal, dhrupada-dhamar, tarana* and *thumri* is called *chou-mukha*.

It is interesting to note that a medieval musical form known as *chaturmukha* and *chaturanga,* a contemporary form possibly derived from the former includes elements that are predominant in the four forms mentioned above: meaningful words *(khayal)*, sol-fa singing *(sargam)*, meaningless auspicious syllables *(tarana)*.

It is presumed that a female singer displaying similar capacity would need a similar term!

1.3.5 *Dhrupadiya* (H *dhrupad* + suffix *ya*)

Dhrupadiya is a male singer specializing in the performance of the musical form known as *dhrupad*. It is to be marked that the *ya*-ending formation is restricted to only two forms, namely, *khayal* and *dhrupad*. If the reasons are not linguistic, the fact may prove the predominance of the two forms within the art-music repertoire of vocal modality.

1.3.6 *Gandharva* (S)

Gandharva means a celestial musician, a class of demi-gods regarded as the singers or musicians of gods and said to have 'good voices agreeable to females'. An interesting etymological explanation states that *dha* suggests drinking and those who sing while drinking are known as *gandharva*s!

The term has a long history. In ancient India during various periods the term *gandharva* was applied to:

1   deities who knew divine secrets,
2   demi-gods who specialized in preparing *soma*, the divine drink and who were partial to women,
3   those who (in addition to being inclined towards wine and women) were court-musicians to Indra, the king of gods.

In later history a particular region was associated with them, a fact which would probably suggest that they were caste-musicians.

From medieval times onwards, *gandharva*s were those who knew the ancient as well as the modern vocal and instrumental music.

Today the term has been equated with sweetness in singing and is used as an honorific.

1.3.7 *Gayaka* (S *gai* = to sing)

It may mean:

1   one who is singing,
2   one who earns livelihood by singing,
3   one who sings praises (of a patron).

As a term, *gayaka* is a value-neutral description of a performer who uses voice as his medium. Of the three meanings noted above, the first suggests a vocalist, that is, a maker of music through voice. The second shade suggests a professional status (as opposed to an amateur). The third refers to a class of performers appointed to sing compositions in praise of kings, patrons etc.

A female vocalist is described as *gayika*. If performers are referred to as *ganewala* and *ganewali*, there is a slide-down in the social scale. The terms connote performers from a lower class of professional entertainers of easy virtue.

The medieval musicological tradition had a five-fold classification of *gayaka*s as shown below:

shikshakar	=	a conscientious and able teacher.
anukar	=	an able imitator.
rasik	=	one who sang with emotion.
ranjak	=	an entertainer.
bhavak	=	an innovator capable of revitalizing music.

1.3.8 *Gavaiyya* (H *gana* = to sing)
The term is understood as a special continuation of the term *gayaka*. A male art-musician of recognized mastery over the science and practice of music is called *gavaiyya*.

1.3.9 *Guni/gunakar* (S possessor of qualities)
Generally it refers to one acquainted with the current as opposed to ancient music and one who can perform it proficiently.

1.3.10 *Kalavant* (S *kalavan* = one who knows art)
The historian Abul Fazl (1551-96) described a professional singer of *dhrupad* as *kalavant* and added that such singers come from a caste which makes its living from music. In Rajasthan, *kalavant* denotes a caste-musician and a folk performer who sings but does not play an instrument. He also eschews dancing.

It is in this perspective that art-musicians took umbrage on being described as *kalavant*s. In 1937 they registered an organized protest on being described as *kalavant*s!

Today the term has become almost harmless as it is taken to mean 'an artiste'.

1.3.11 *Kalakar/Kalavati* (S *kala* = art)
Refer to a male or female artiste respectively. Etymologically there is no justification to confine the terms to music. Both are general terms covering all modalities, forms etc. in music.

1.3.12 *Khayaliya* (H *khayal* + suffix *ya*)
A male singer who specializes in rendering the Hindustani vocal form *khayal*, is called a *khyaliya*. The *ya* ending is restricted to only two forms, namely *khayal* and *dhrupad* and to that extent the prominence of the two forms within the Hindustani repertoire is emphasized.

1.3.13 *Mirashi* or *Mirasi* (A)
Mirashi or *mirasi* is a caste term. One who accompanies courtesans or 'nautch' girls on string or membrane-covered instruments, is described as *mirashi* or *mirasi*. Muslim caste-musicians residing in Punjab were also described as *mirashi*. Females in the caste, known as *mirasins*, are professional performers.

Today the term has come to mean an inferior musician accompanying a vocalist. Music education imparted by a *mirashi* is looked down upon. It is expected to be less authentic and less scientific.

1.3.14 *Nayaka* (S one who rules over others)
1   a male musician from a caste known for training others in music and dance.
2   a person well-versed in the theory and practice of music.
The latter, less derogatory meaning is more prevalent.

1.3.15 *Pandit* (S a learned person)
A person well-versed in the theory of music.

1.3.16 *Peshewar* (< P *peshvar*)
One who renders professionally in front of, in the presence of others.
1.3.17 *Qawwal* (A *kaul* = aphorism, saying)
One who sings *quawwali* songs.

1.3.18 *Shoukin* (A)
A person who studies or does something repeatedly to get joy out of the activity.

In music, *shoukin* means one who loves, studies and practices some kind of music with recognizable competence but does not enter the fray as a full-fledged musician. In all probability, a *shoukin* musician does not earn his living from music though he performs seriously and offers patronage to music and musicians generously. Compared to *peshewar*-musicians, a *shoukin* or an amateur is judged less rigorously. He enjoys more affection than respect from the hard-core performers!

1.3.19 *Vadaka* (S *vad* = to sound)
A performer who plays some instrument to make music is known as a
vadaka. He may or may not do so as an accompanist. The term does
not suggest any specific musical instrument nor does it suggest any
socio-musicological status.

1.3.20 *Vyavasayika* (H < S *vyavasaya* = business, employment,
profession)
A professional performer as distinguished from an amateur, is
known as *vyavasayika*. Not only is he supposed to earn his livelihood
through performance but (more importantly) he is also expected to
maintain high standards in effectiveness, proficiency, width of repertoire etc. Demands made on a *vyavasayika* musician are in all
respects more exacting. Sometimes, *peshewar* is used as synonym for
vyavasayika and vice versa.

1.4 Accompaniment
In the Hindustani system, music-making is predominantly a solo activity. It is the individual performer who enjoys freedom and scope to
project and elaborate his musical ideas. However the help of accompanists of different kinds and the varying degrees of their participa-
tion is not entirely denied to him. In fact for most of the performances in Hindustani music there is a performing set which consists of
three components, namely, the main artiste/s, the accompanist/s and
the audience.

In Hindustani music accompaniment is of three kinds: melodic,
rhythmic and the drone.

The melodic accompaniment is on the tonal axis and in essence it
concentrates on progression of pitches used in music. The rhythmic accompaniment focuses on beats as time-divisions and their patterns.
The drone provides a continuous fundamental, the pitch-base on which
a musician constructs his selected scale upwards and downwards. Of
the three the drone is the more constant. The other two are variables
in the sense that if the main artiste so chooses, improvised interrup-
tions, link-phrases in melodic and rhythmic accompaniments may find
a place. However the basic tenet is that by intention and arrangement,
accompanists are followers, not leaders.

The distribution of the accompanying set reflects in a way the
primacy of vocal music. For example, the following may be
noted:

Main artiste	Accompaniment
Vocalist	rhythmic, melodic and the drone
Instrumentalist (rhythm)	melodic and drone
Instrumentalist (melody)	rhythmic and drone

While describing the desirability of musical instruments, Sharangdeva, the medieval musicologist, made an admission of rare candour. He stated that rhythm instruments enthuse, encourage and bring joy to those in pain. . . and then added 'all instruments help in concealing the shortcomings of the artiste'. It is obvious that the accompanists may find themselves engaged in this musical philanthropy oftener than could be imagined!

1.4.1 *Lehra* (H *leher* = ripple, small wave)
For solo performances on rhythm instruments, especially on *tabla* as also in solo dance items, a recurring tonal pattern encompassing a predetermined number of beats is supplied cyclically in the required tempo on *sarangi*, harmonium, violin or on some such on melodic instrument. The repeated melodic pattern is known as *lehra*.

The essence of a *lehra* is its constancy; it is not elaborated though the *lehra* player may tend to add a few embellishments occasionally. It is untiringly presented as a reference circle to the solo-player as per his directions. It truly constitutes a minor musical wave!

1.4.2 *Sazinda* (P *saz* = instrument)
An accompanist on a tonal or rhythmic instrument. Reportedly, the term indicates low status of the accompanists as they play with courtesans etc.

1.4.3 *Sangatiya* (H S *sam* = *together* + *gam* = to go)
Sangat indicates a purposeful coming together of two entities which can otherwise be independent of each other.

In sophisticated musicological parlance *sangat* means accompaniment, not by repeating what the chief musician has done nor is it a mechanical imitation of the soloist. In essence *sangat* is to provide a tonal or a rhythmic complement to the main artiste, suitably and attractively matching or responding to his expression. In case the accompanist chooses to follow the soloist mechanically, his contribution is described as *sath* which merely means 'to be with'.

The term is not to be confused with *sangati*, though both the terms are etymologically connected. In music *sangati* is a special relationship of agreement between two or more tonal phrases or patterns positionally placed at a fair distance from one another and preferably in different halves of the scale-space.

1.4.4 *Sath* (H < S *sahit* = with)
Sath connotes a type of imitative and less creative accompaniment to the main artiste. (Also see *Sangat*).

1.4.5 *Sur* (H < S *swara* = note)
The drone accompaniment which characterizes Hindustani art music of both vocal and instrumental modalities is known as *sur*. A drone basically supplies a continuous fundamental in the scale selected by the performer. Sometimes, the fifth of the fundamental and the lower octave are also included in the *sur*. Considered as a whole, the *sur* turns out to be more of an atmospheric agent than a mere supply of one basic note etc. *Tanpura* for vocal music, *tamburi* for string instruments etc., *sur* for *shehnai, sruti*-box or harmonium are some other examples of *surs*.

Drone provides *adharswara*, that is the note which serves as a foundation to music-making. The principle of tonality (fixing the fundamental) and regarding *shadja, pancham* as immovable notes played important roles in determining the character of the sur as it obtains today.

Usages such as *sur dena* (to give a *sur*) or *sur bharna* (to fill a *sur*) suggest the elements of continuity and fullness any *sur* should necessarily possess.

1.4.6 *Talapani* (S *tal* = to fix, found, establish *tala* = clapping, slapping + *pani* = hands)
It is a useful term. Unfortunately it has gone out of circulation. A person who provides accompaniment by marking *tala* by handclaps is called *talapani*. He may or may not recite the *tala* syllables aloud. Even today a *talapani* is seen in action in a *pakhwaj* solo. It is of interest to note that *talapani* is not in action with *tabla* etc., these being modern compared to the *pakhwaj*, the drum of ancient origin.

1.4.7 *Talapachara* (S *tala* = rhythm + *apachara* = departure)
A person who provides rhythm accompaniment to control a procession etc. by marking *tala* with hand-claps and by reciting the *tala*-syllables aloud, is called a *talapachara*, meaning literally 'to walk with *tala*'.

1.5 Forms of music

The term 'form' is used in two senses. A wider and a more concep-
tual sense is indicated when we judge a particular performance of
music as 'formless'. It may be marked by lack of a sense of direction;
the expression may be irregular in construction; the components may
suffer from a lack of equilibrium leading one to remark 'there is no
form in this entire activity'. On the other hand the performance may
reveal a definite sequence; the expression may display a purposeful
selection of modes of performing; the arrangement of components
may exihibit an application of unambiguous criteria leading one to
conclude that the performance was, for example, of vocal, classical,
khayal music. This latter judgement indicates appreciation of a form
of music.

This section is concerned with the narrower sense of the term 'form'
which focuses on forms of music. The concept of form is immediately
related to the important aesthetic issues of form and content, ex-
perience and conception as well as that of tradition and innovation.
However the discussion is pitched at a less ambitious level, that of explaining the contemporary vogue of music obtained in the customary
musical situations such as concert, practice and learning.

If vocal and instrumental musical repertoires are considered
together, the number of music-forms does not exceed fifty! This is
surprising because the medieval musicological scene could boast of at
least seventy-five. The late eighteenth century chroniclers of musical
practice enumerated about thirty-five forms of music.

However the attrition is deceptive. Firstly the contemporary
categorization of music into primitive, folk, art and popular was not applied earlier and secondly the segregation of arts into literary, performing and the fine arts too is a recent attempt. Unlike in the medieval discussion of music, a ritualistic dance-music might be considered
nowadays as folk. Similarly, today a poem in which each line is composed in a different language may be considered a form of literature,
and not of music. This is no place to lay down the theoretical principles
that govern the crystallization of music into forms of art-music.
However it would be helpful though somewhat simplistic to state that
accent on tonal or rhythmic material, emphasis on meaningful or intellectual patterning and importance of simplicity of statement or complexity of rendering seem to provide the criteria relevant to performance as well as appreciation of music.

1.5.1 *Arya*

Arya does not enjoy the status of musical form suited to concert stage. It is one of the singable and ancient metres regulated by the number of syllabic instants. It was pressed into service to string together coherently the grammatical features of *raga* etc. The flexible structure of the arya has obvious musical possibilities. It is no accident that it was used in the famous collection of songs in *Maharashtra Prakrit* of King Hala. With its many metrical variants *arya* is abundantly sung by *keertankar*s in the *Naradiya* tradition even today.

1.5.2 *Bandish* (H binding together)

The literal meaning does not reflect the qualitative musical distinction the term connotes. Any musical composition, or a *cheez* as it is called, is not accorded the status of a *bandish*. A *bandish* is a composition which, due to its inherent completeness, can claim to be a map of a full musical growth, a complete form in a seed. Hence a performer who establishes his mastery of *bandish* is immediately accepted by the knowledgeable. Indian musicians, rightly, lay emphasis on knowing as many of *bandish*s as possible. In fact a musician who scores high in this respect is described with a special adjective *kothiwale* (a veritable store house).

1.5.3 *Bhajan* (H *bhaj* = to serve)

It may be recalled that the all-encompassing devotional movement sweeping over the country from the eighth century gave music a place of importance. The result was a burgeoning of song, dance and drama. A number of song-types crystallized into musical structures of immense variety, according to the regional genius and linguistic-literary traditions. When such song-types are employed (with or without ritualistic context) as items in musico-devotional acts they can be brought under the generic term *bhajan*.

A unique category of composers are responsible for this type of music. They are aptly described in India as saint-poets. Almost every region in India produced a galaxy of them; and, as a rule, they were prolific composers. Some of their compositions are still in circulation as *bhajan*s and presented as such on the concert stage. The saint poets employed definite *raga*s and *tala*s; however, the tunes they used are not necessarily current today. Some constructional features of a *bhajan* may be noted:

Pad: The meaningful, literary stanzas in the *bhajan*s which are generally short in length.

Biruda: A salutation to the deity etc.

Tek: The unit formed by the first two lines. This is generally repeated after every stanza in case of a multistanza composition. It may be called the refrain of the song.

Mudra: The name of the composer usually included in the last line of a *bhajan*.

Examined musically the traditional *bhajan*-tunes are found to employ repeatedly, certain *raga*-scales, such as, *desh, sarang, bhairav, kalingda, mand, kalyan* and *malhar*. Preponderence of regional melodies (e.g. *mand*), seasonal melodies (e.g. *malhar*) and those from the ancient six ragas (e.g. *bhairav*) is significant. A similar usage is detected in various folk musical traditions in India. The similarities go a long way in explaining the hold of the devotional and the folk categories on people in general. *Bhajans* employ rhythms with eight or sixteen beats. The tempo is neither slow nor fast. A gradual increase in the tempo towards musical climax is a general characteristic.

The instrumentation displays preference for one/two stringed instruments which function as drone-cum-rhythm providers. Struck, rather than scraped percussive instruments are favourites. For example *jhanj, manjiri, chipli, daph, dimdi* would come to mind.

It is obvious that *bhajans* were originally meant to be solo/choral renderings in homes and temples. Their concert appearance is a comparatively recent phenomenon traceable to the early years of the twentieth century.

1.5.4 *Chaturanga* (H < S *chatur* = four + *rang* = colour)

It is an inclusive form consisting of meaningful words, meaningless sound-clusters, letters indicating note-names and sound-clusters selected from those used in *pakhawaj* elaborations. In the medieval tradition a similar form was known as *chaturmukh*, that is, 'one having four mouths'.

Now rarely rendered, *chaturang* has a definite value as a musical curiosity though its musical potential is limited. It is sung in medium to fast tempo and uses *ragas* circulating in the *khayal* (>) corpus.

1.5.5 *Chaiti* (H < S *chaitra* = the first month of the Hindu calender)

Folk songs in Uttar Pradesh and adjacent areas sung in the month of *chaitra* are called *chaiti*. Special constructional features include beginning of line with the word *Rama* and ending it with *ho Rama*. When sung to the accompaniment of instruments, *chaiti* is known as *jhalkutiya*.

In the semi-art musical repertoire *chaiti* has now acquired a place. Musically it follows the formulae used in *thumri* (>) singing. In other words, efforts are made to employ evocative tunes, tones and temperaments. Thematically *chaiti* centres on describing pangs of separation.

1.5.6 *Cheez* (H thing, item)

Cheez is a composition in vocal classical music. Its main components are meaningful words with a definite *raga*-structure and use of a particular *tala*. Unlike *bandish* (>), *cheez*, as a concept, is less value-oriented.

1.5.7 *Dadra*

Primarily *dadra* denotes a *tala* (>) of six beats. However *dadra* also refers to a form of semi-art music in *dadra tala* with the characteristic lilt of the *tala* neatly emphasized.

Set to tune in *dhun-ragas* (>) employed usually in *thumri*-singing, *dadra* is invariably linked with the thumri as *dhamar* (>) is with *dhrupada* (>). In fact it would not be farfetched to suggest that forms named after *talas* indicate their subsidiary position in the heirarchy of forms. In tone, tune and temperament *dadras* are fittingly paired with *thumris*.

1.5.8 *Dhamar*

Primarily denotes a *tala* (>) of fourteen beats. However *dhamar* is also a form of *dhrupada* (>) sung in *dhamar tala*. After a *dhrupada* has been presented, *dhamar* is to be rendered in a tempo faster than that of the *dhrupada*. Contentwise, *dhamar* is secular and is often inclined towards mild eroticism.

1.5.9 *Doha* (n. H < S *dohad,* or *dwipad,* indicating two units)

Primarily a metre with a stanza of four lines, its alternate lines have thirteen and eleven letters.

Doha is of musical interest because it has been conventionally employed to codify grammatical rules and norms of music condensed aphoristically. They are usually couched in Brij and Prakrit languages of north India. Musicians memorize and quote them often.

1.5.10 *Dhrupada* (H < S *dhruva* = firm, stable, unshareable, *pada* = stanza, place or position)

Dhrupada refers to the burden of the poem in prosody. It remains unchanged and occurs repeatedly. It is logical that the term is also used to denote the place of God. Combining the two semantic thrusts, *dhrupada* has come to mean a composition in praise of God. Against this background, *dhrupada* is to be understood today as a form of Hindustani art-music venerated for its long history and divine association.

An unambiguous evidence of its prosperity places it in the fifteenth century despite the tantalizing traces from the earlier period. Legendary figures such as Baiju Bawara, Gopal, Tansen are named as its main performers. Going back a little, the term *dhruva* is found to have been employed in *Geetgovind* with reference to the first two lines of a stanza, the rest being described as *pad*. In the medieval *Sangit Ratnakara*, a compositional genre called *dhruva prabandha* is specified in great detail. The structural features as laid down there establish a clear link between the contemporary *dhrupada* and its proto-type in the *Ratnakara*.

The four structural features or parts of *dhrupada* as stabilized today are:

Name	Function
Sthayi	to begin a composition and establish its *raga*.
Antara	to follow immediately after the *sthayi* and explore the *raga*, usually accentuating the upper half of the scale in the process.
Abhog	to give a sense of completion and to round-off.
Sanchari	free movement.

The form follows a performing sequence with a marked strictness.

Singing of a *dhrupada* commences with *nom-tom*. Meaningless syllables such as *ri, da, na, nom, tom, yala, li* etc. are employed in the *nom-tom* to unfold the *raga* in slow, medium and fast tempo without the use of song-text and *tala*. It has been occasionally argued that *nom-tom* employs in reality the auspicious *mantra*-phrase *anant hari om* with tonal patterns superimposed on them and hence the words can hardly be called meaningless though they may be truncated or distorted during the performance. It is to be admitted however that a majority of musicians do not seem to use these or such other words. Historical prespective suggests *nom-tom* to be an extension of the medieval concept of employing meaningless syllables as auspicious words. The usage was then known as *tena-shabda*.

After the *non-tom*, comes the second phase in the singing of *dhrupada*. Here, the four parts described earlier are sung in *tala* to the accompaniment of *pakhawaj*(>), a horizontal two-faced drum. In the third phase the song-text is sung in double, treble and quadruple tempi. Finally, improvised renderings of the texts are introduced in varied, changing tempi. A variety of tonal patterns are also put forward. Conventionally, the *dhrupada* eschews singing in bare vowels and denies singers the luxury of *tans*(>).

Traditional *dhrupada*s when examined for their thematic content seem to prefer praise of gods, kings, descriptions of nature etc. In other words the non-personal and the semi-religious elements are to the fore. The versification is serious in tone. The usual tempo (described by the term *vilambit*) is slow. It is deliberately increased to medium-fast while moving towards the climax. The conventional singing is virile and manly: it is rare to come across a female *dhrupada* performer.

Dhrupada mostly employs *choutal* (12 beats), *soorfakta* (10 beats), and *adital* (16 beats). Almost all the traditional *ragas* find place. In fact the coextensiveness of the form and the *raga*-set has been so close in the tradition that one test of the authenticity of a *raga* is supposed to be availability of a *dhrupada* in it!

From the aesthetic point of view *dhrupada* lacks in flexibility because of the prescriptive syntax of the elaboration phases as well as the rather artificial bifurcation between the tonal and the rhythmic aspects. Significantly, *dhrupada* is traditionally followed by *dhamar*(>) which does away with some of the restrictions reigning in *dhrupada* singing. (Also see *sadra, vishnupad, langda dhrupada*.)

1.5.11 *Geet* (H = that which is sung)
A composition characterized by tune, metre, rhythm and language is *geet*. The traditional terminology describes *matukara* as one who drafts the linguistic composition. One who takes care of tune and rhythm is known as *dhatukara*. The rare person able to take care of both is called *vaggeyakara*. On the other hand a person versifying to match a tune already composed is known as *kuttikara*. The last variety is granted a lower status.

An important classification of the form introduced by the musicological tradition stresses the overall rhythmic-melodic orientation of a *geet*. Those with a rhythmic weightage were called *padashrita* (dependent on language-units), while those emphasizing the melodic aspect were named *swarashrita* (dependent on notes).

It is to be regretted that the traditional theoretical positions about *geet* are not in easy circulation. Today any lyric/poem sung to a certain tune, with or without the applications of *raga/tala* or such other concepts in art-music is described as a *geet*. The term has obviously become more accomodative, literature-oriented and less precise than suggested by the traditional musicology.

1.5.12 *Ghazal* (P a love-song)

The original meaning of the term was a love song in Persian. Later, the Urdu literary tradition while deriving inspiration from the Persian continuity, extended the thematic range and admitted *ghazal*s touching on other subjects. More specifically *kasida* in Persian literature was the precursor of *ghazal*. (Literally, *ghazal* means to talk of love with women.) From the beginning of the tradition, love of God was also a strand of the thematic fabric of the form. The *sufi*s were responsible for the early prosperity *ghazal*s enjoyed. The *sufi*s registered a presence at Aurangabad in Maharashtra during the early ninth century.

On account of the metrical conventions as well as norms governing other structural features, *ghazal* certainly puts restrictions on the use of *tala*s. The literary genesis of the form is proclaimed by its prosodic features which in turn influence the rhythmic framework employed. It is no surprise that *ghazal*s continued to be associated with *mushaira*s (poet's conferences) in which poetry is recited.

There is evidence to suggest that till the 1920s, *ghazal* was sung almost as a *tappa* (>). From the earlier recitation-phase this was surely a step ahead but the non-correspondence between the romantically inclined content and the intellectual intricacy of *tappa*-singing, warranted a change. Gradually however the *ghazal* came to be sung to the accompaniment of instruments *a la thumri* (>). At this stage some musical embellishment was introduced, yet no musical elaboration was expected or attempted, even though certain *raga*s seem to recur in the tunes employed. Today both *raga*-orientation and musical elaboration are on the increase.

Constructional features that have a bearing on singing of a *ghazal* are:

1	*beher*	metre
2	*radif*	end rhyme
3	*kafiya*	word preceding the end-rhyme
4	*misra*	line

5	sher	couplet
6	ashar	a number of *shers*
7	katah	*ashar*, brought together thematically
8	matla	first *sher*
9	makta	last *sher*
10	takhallus	*nom de plume*
11	husn-e-matla	the most important *sher*

A non-rhythmic singing of *sher* in the *ghazal* presentation is often introduced on the spur of the moment. *Matla* is repeated often. End-rhymes are emphasized and *misra* is placed in varied tonal contexts.

1.5.13 Holi/hori (H < S Holika, meaning a spring festival)

It is a song akin to *dhrupada* (>) set in principal *ragas* with love-pranks of Radha and Krishna as the main theme. *Dhamar tala* is used in most cases. Alternatively, other *talas* such as *jhumra* and *deepchandi* (which too have fourteen beats) are also used. On account of the importance given to the *dhamar tala*, *hori* is also known as *dhamar* (>).

If the theme of the composition is the colour-festival known as *holi* in India, *holi* is to be included in the *thumri* (>) group of semi-classical forms; otherwise the pronounced *dhrupad*-orientation is to be recognized for classification.

Holi, as a festival, is known for the celebration which includes kindling of the sacred fire symbolizing the burning of the demoness Holika. Alternatively it alludes to the burning of Madan, Lord of Love, by Shiva whose penance Madan disturbed. *Holi* is celebrated on the full moon day of *Phalgun* in the Hindu calendar.

1.5.14 Kajli/kajri (H kajal = eye black)

It is a female folk-song from Uttar Pradesh and adjacent region, sung in the rainy season. It has many, different tunes.

On the third day in the second half of *Bhadra*, women sing *kajli*-songs all through the night to an accompanying circle-dance.

As a form in semi-art music, *kajli* has found a place along with *chaiti* (>). Both are alike in many respects.

However, as a form of popular music, *kajli* has developed another variety more deliberately processed and formalised. This type of *kajli*s are composed and taught by expert *ustad*s to professional singing women called *gounharin*s. Each *ustad*'s school is known as *akhada* (i.e. a meeting place of professional entertainers). Competitive persentations of the *kajli*s are made by organized and trained parties pitted against one another on occasions described as *dangal*s.

The opposing parties are seated on two platforms facing one another. *Dholak*, the main accompanying rhythm instrument, is worshipped. One of the *ustad*s then stands up and sings in praise of God (*sumran*). The competing party follows in the same metre and the thematic question-answers continue. To the accompaniment of the *dholak, chang* and *lakadi* etc., the *kajli dangal* continues through the night. By sunrise the parties are locked in the last phase of the musical combat in which personal and obscene attacks (*phataha*) as well as extempore compositions called *baradasta* are prominently employed to compel the opposition to admit defeat.

1.5.15 *Khayal* (H song, A idea)

The etymology is confusing. Some scholars maintain that it is related to the folk repertoire of Rajasthan. However the *khayal* in Rajasthan is of many kinds, the common feature being a package that brings dance, drama and music together. The *khayal* under discussion is entirely a vocal presentation.

Some others derive *khayal* from *khel* (H < S *krida* = play).

Obviously a reference to the greater freedom of elaboration allowed in *khayal* is intended. A contrast to the rigid sequences of *dhrupad* (>) is also brought into relief because *dhrupad* is reported to have made room for the *khayal* during the sixteenth century.

History

Amir Khusro (1254-1325) and alternatively, Sultan Hussain Sharki of Jaunpur (1457-1476) have been credited as creators of *khayal*.

The composer 'Sadarang' Nyamatkhan in the court of Mohammad Shah (1719-1748) is stated to have popularized the *khayal*. It is interesting that the medieval *Sangit Ratnakara* mentions a not very prestigious new form of music, *khallotara* and frowns on it as one that alters (distorts!) characteristics of established *raga*s and *kavya* (poetry). A question arises: is *khallotara* a Sanskritization of *khayal*?

However that may be, the present-day *khayal* is the result of a cumulative process of musical liberalization in matters current for at least four centuries before *khayal* attained a new stability in the hands of the composer 'Sadarang' Nyamtkhan.

Structure

Today *khayal* features two *tuk*s (parts), namely, *sthayi* and *antara* as contrasted with the four parts of the *dhrupada*. The first part called *sthayi* usually covers the first half of the gamut and the second half, *antara*, mainly explores the upper ranges. Together the two are expected to explore the total *raga*-frame. A composition of one single part was, according to Capt. Willard, known as *chutkula*. In case a *khayal* has three parts, the one between *sthayi* and *antara* is known as *manja* (middle, intervening). Each separate line of a *khayal* is called a *charan*. Usually a *khayal* does not have more than four or six lines, but there is no rigid rule about it. The oft-repeated, and important part of the first line of a *khayal* is called *mukhda* (S dim. of *mukh* = face). All the words used in a *khayal* are collectively known as *bol* (words).

Definition

Khayal may be defined as a form of Hindustani vocal art music in which a song is composed in a definite *raga* to be sung in a *tala*.

The singing of a *khayal* however does not mean singing the *khayal* composition. Unless the composition is elaborated further a *khayal* does not attain its full stature. The usual plan of presenting an elaborate *khayal* may include the following phases:

a   Initial singing of *sthayi* and *antara*. This is designed to establish the range, mood and nature of the *raga*.

b   *Alap:* Slow-tempo spelling out of the various melodic ideas contained in a *raga*. Each *alap* terminates with the *mukhda* and a new one begins. There is no limit to the number of *tala* cycles an *alap* requires. Employing the *mukhda* and coming to the *sam,* the first beat of the *tala*-cycle, indicates the completion of *alap* as a statement of the musical idea. Usually the vowel-sound 'a' is used to sing the *alap*.

c   *Bol-alap:* the phase combines *alap* and enunciation of words of the composition concerned. This is expected to add one more dimension to the elaboration, because meaningfulness of the words becomes a potential force in shaping the musical idea. The words and notes together afford a qualitatively different take-off even as sound-clusters.

d   *Bol-lay:* Instead of combining *bols* with *alaps* they can also be brought into relief as units of rhythmic patterns without disturbing the *raga*-frame. The *bols* themselves would offer a rhythmic quality when treated as sound-clusters. The *bol-lay* phase pays deliberate attention to stressing of *bols* to create rhythmic patterns. The phase thus succeeds in highlighting a different aspect of words.

e   *Bol-tan:* This phase is marked by an alliance of words with fast tempo melodic progressions known as *tans* (>).

f   *Tan* is usually the climatic phase. Fast tempo tonal patterns (ideally) ranging over three octaves seem a natural climax to music-making. On account of the accent on speed and the creation of varied patterns within the relevant *raga*-scale, *tans* function as instantaneous recapitulations of *ragas*. It is to be noted that *tans* are not confined to *khayal*. They are musical highpoints and are therefore employed liberally in all musical categories. They fulfill a performing need.

The six phases outlined so far do not constitute rigid divisions and music enjoys their inevitable overlapping *avatars*! Yet they differ in qualitative impacts and one cannot be confused for the other. A *khayal* sung in a slow tempo has a natural capacity to accomodate all the phases comfortably. Such a *khayal* is therefore known as *bada* (great) *khayal.*

A *bada khayal* is generally followed by another short piece in the same *raga* but (in most cases) in a different *tala*. This is known as a *chhota* (small) *khayal.* Sung in a faster tempo the *chhota khayal* affords more scope for *bol tan* and *tan.*

A less general and a rather atavistic practice is to sing *khayal* in *madhyalaya* (that is, medium tempo). From such a *khayal* accrues the advantage of employing features of both the *bada* and the *chhota khayals* as it suits the musician.

A person who emphasizes the *tan*-phase in greater proportion is known as a *tanait* and his music is described as *tanaiti.*

1.5.16 *Lakshangeet* (H < S *lakshan* = characterstic + *geet* = song)

A *lakshangeet* is a composition versifying the musicological features of a raga set to tune in the *raga* it describes. Obviously *lakshangeet* has more educational utility than musical potentiality.

Pandit V. N. Bhatkhande (1860-1937) was the first major authority to take *lakshangeet* seriously. He not only composed them but varied the content. In his *lakshangeet* compositions, one finds three varieties. The first describes the characteristics of a *raga* and is composed in the same *raga*. The second kind of *lakshangeet* discusses theoretical issues in musicology and uses the question and answer structure. Finally there are some dealing with the characteristics of *tala*.

Pandit Govindrao Tembe (1881-1955), a wellknown harmonium player, composer, playwright, writer on music and an actor-singer groomed in the Jaipur gharana composed *lakshangeet*s which are poetic both in form and substance. They are easier to render in a concert. In them *raga*-characteristics are described but poetic craft is employed to diminish the effects of a bone-dry grammatical statement.

1.5.17 *Langda dhrupada* (H *langda* = lame + *dhrupada* (>))
Langda dhrupada is a class of compositions which tries to avoid the rigidity of *dhrupada* and the extreme flexibility of *khayal* (>). *The most noticeable feature in a langda dhrupada* is that the words do not follow the *tala*-beats strictly though the tendency to recognize the main divisions of the *tala* is unmistakable. On the other hand a *khayal* moves freely in the *tala*-frame.

1.5.18 *Qawwali* (H A *kaul* = aphorism, saying)
Originally *qawwalis* were songs in praise of God. It was also customary to pair together *qawwali* and *kalbana,* both being concerned the same theme.

Later the form came to include compositions in Persian.

In India *qawwali* stabilized around the thirteenth century and the *sufi*s enlisted its services to spread their message. Amir Khusro, a *sufi* and an innovator contributed to the vogue of the form. Those who sang *kaul* and *tarana* (>) were known as *qawwalbacche* (sons of *qawwali*-singers). A disputed tradition traces the performing dominance of *khayal* (>) to the *qawwalbacche.*

The contemporary practice suggests that *qawwali* is a mode of singing rather than a form of composition. A kind of *ghazal* (>) when treated in a particular mode becomes *qawwali.* With a little simplification it may be said that while a *ghazal* dealing with the theme of love is rendered in the *ghazal*-way, that which centres on the love of God is presented as a *qawwali.*

In performance, *qawwali* presents a fascinating, interchanging use of the solo and the choral modalities. Usually *qawwali* is sung by a party (and two parties if the event is competitive). One or two singers are the chief presenters and they are provided with a vocal support (of two or more persons), rhythmic support (*dholak, tabla, khanjiri* and prominently handclaps) and melodic support (on harmonium and *bulbultarang*— the latter is a curious keyboard string instrument).

1.5.19 *Sadra*

A *dhrupada* (>) or a *hori* (>) composed in *jhaptal,* a *tala* of ten beats, is called *sadra.* Tradition has it that two composer brothers, Shivmohan and Shivnath, followers of the style of the legendary Baiju Bawra, hailed from Shahadra and the form derives its name from this place-name.

Alternatively it is said that *sadra* corresponds to *gurcha,* a song-type in Rajasthani language. The latter composition-type in praise of valorous deeds is characterized by long running lines. *Sadra* is in the *brij* dialect.

1.5.20 *Sargamgeet* (H *saragam* = note names of the Indian musical scale + *geet* = song)

Even though taught and practiced in traditional music-teaching, it was rarely sung in concerts. However *sargamgeet* enjoys the advantages of meaninglessness (*a la tarana*) and also presents the *raga*-image with fidelity. It remains a mystery why *sargamgeet* has not caught the fancy of enterprising vocalists, especially because *raga*-elaboration in varied tempi along with use of *sargam* has already become prevalent. It is merely a step away from bestowing concert status on *sargamgeet.*

Medieval performing tradition had a form named *swarartha* (notes with meaning): the term is a tribute to the medieval sensibility!

1.5.21 *Sawan* (H S *shravan* = a month in the rainy season)

A form of semi-classical song sung in the rainy season. It describes the rainy season and the pangs of separation conventionally associated with it in India.

Basically *sawan* uses varieties of *Malhar, Desh* etc. and *ardhatala*s such as *keharawa, dadra* etc.

A variety of *sawan* songs sung while sitting on a swing is known as *sawan-hindola.* It is sung by women and the theme is love.

1.5.22 *Tarana, trivat, ras* and *khayal-numa/nama*

The repertoire of Hindustani art music boasts of a number of forms that combine meaningful words and meaningless sound-clusters, the latter usually borrowed from the 'language' of rhythm and string instruments. A contributory convention is to regard specific (otherwise meaningless) sound-clusters as specially and mystically auspicious.

It is against this background that the four forms grouped together in the entry need to be understood.

1.5.23 *Tarana* (H *taranah*)
Essentially a composition consisting of sound-syllables of rhythm and string instruments (excluding those of the *pakhawaj*). Sung in medium or fast tempo, *tarana* relies on fast elaborations known as *tans* (>) for its impact. Ordinarily it has two parts known as *sthayi* (>) and *antara* (>). The form does not restrict itself to any particular *tala* and is found in almost all *ragas*.

Tradition credits Amir Khusro (1253-1325) for having combined the Farsi *rubai* (a poetic form of aphoristic couplets) with the then prevailing modes of employing meaningless sound-clusters to shape *tarana*. The usual sound-clusters encountered in a *tarana* are *dir dir, ta na, na na, yalali, lom, ni, tom* etc. In this context the medieval tradition of combining *tena shabda* (meaningless syllables regarded as auspicious) and the *patashabda* (the instrumental sounds) needs to be remembered.

1.5.24 *Trivat*
Similar to the *tarana* in most respects, except that it employs sound-clusters of the *pakhawaj* (>). The latter are more rotund and sonorous compared to those used in *tarana*. For example, *tak ghidan, dhir dhir kidtak, didnag, ghidnag, tak kadan* etc. are noteworthy.

1.5.25 *Ras* (H < S *ras* = to create a din)
1   Kind of dance practised by Krishna and his cowherd companions, but particularly the *gopis*, the milkmaids of Vrindavan. A circular dance and the accompanying song.
2   A rare vocal classical form akin to *tarana*. Differs from the latter because *ras* employs meaningless sound-clusters used in the rhythm-language of dance : example, *ta thaiya, thun, thun* etc.

1.5.26 *Khayal-numa/nama* (A H *khayal* + P *numa* = according to)
Numa is a suffix that points to something not directly presented in the word. Hence the form under discussion indicates *khayal* (>) which in reality is not presented in the composition. *Khayal-numa* employs meaningless sound-clusters as in *tarana* but in a tempo which reminds one of a *khayal*. It is clear that the luxury to elaborate (because of the slow tempo) and the freedom from the constraints of language (because of the meaninglessness) constitute the special attractions of the form. The name includes distortion of *numa*, the suffix.

1.5.27 *Tapkhayal* (H *tap* = sudden or P *tappa* = to jump + *khayal*)
The form is a result of a resourceful combination of the characteristics of *tappa* (>) and some features of *khayal* (>).

In dynamics, clustering of notes as well as the language selected for the composition *tapkhayal* is mapped on *tappa* (>). It has *sthayi* (>) and *antara* (>) as its parts. It is not restricted to 'lighter' *ragas*. These features are borrowed from *khayal*.

1.5.28 *Tappa* (H *tap* = unexpected, sudden. P *tappa* = jump)
A form in semi-art music reportedly inspired by the folk songs of camel-drivers in the Punjab area.

Couched in Punjabi and Pushtu languages and set in *ragas* generally used for the semi-classical forms, *tappa* is characterized by jumpy and flashy tonal movements.

Embellishments recurring in it are *jamjama, gitkari, khatka* and *murki*. All these exhibit quick movement, imagination, complexity of structure and a dazzling impact. The form proves so attractive that it was combined with *khayal* (>) to produce *tap-khayal* (>).

1.5.28 *Thumri* (H A *thumakna* = to walk with dancing steps so as to make the ankle-bells tinkle)
A semi-classical form of Hindustani vocal music closely associated with dance, dramatic gestures, mild eroticism, evocative love poetry and folk songs of Uttar Pradesh.

History
The proto-type of *thumri* has been traced to *Harivamsha* (400 A. D.) which describes a musical presentation called *chalika*. It combined song with dramatic gestures and dancing movements. Malavika, the heroine of Kalidasa's *Malavikagnimitra* (600 A.D.) is also depicted to have rendered it.

Rajtarangini (1070-1072) of Kalhana deals in great detail with a form called *dombika gayan*, and its similarity with *jhumri* of the later times is striking.

In the medieval *Manasollasa* (1131), *tripadi*, a musical form proscribed from a concert-repertoire, is described as: 'treating themes of love and separation, the three-line composition is sung by women who embellish the song to bring out shades of meaning'.

Further on, *Sangeet Damodara* (1500) refers to a compositional genre called *jhumri*. The description runs thus: 'replete with the love-sentiment, not bound by the constraints of prosodic rules, sweet as a wine, the rhythm-oriented *jhumri* is sung by dancing females'.

The customary credit given to Wajid Ali Shah of Lucknow (1822-1887) for having invented *thumri* flies in the face of history. Capt. Willard in his *Music of India* (1838) mentions many well-known *thumri* singers. Wajid Ali Shah was born in 1822. Obviously the form crystallized over a long period with many practitioners contributing to its development.

Of essence is the fact that all the historical predecessors and musical ancestors of the *thumri* included moderate and suggestive dance-movements, equally restrained *abhinaya* (acting), music as the controlling agent in combination with gentle and feminine eroticism as the moving spirit. The modern *thumri* reached its present state through a natural growth of these various aspects, gradually during the course of history.

Two factors helped in the development of the form.

Firstly, the reigning dynasty in Avadh (capital, Lucknow) was Shia by faith. Hence the rulers were not highly motivated to encourage musical forms such as the *qawwali* (>) with its strong *sufi* associations. On the other hand they were partial to *thumri, chaiti, kajri* etc. as these were based on folk songs prevailing in the region.

Secondly, with many other forms *thumri* also presents a case of successful compromise between monochrome devotionalism and the secular pulls of ordinary life of the people. Secular drive of the life of the senses found an outlet in India through the devotional cults, Krishna-cult being the major channel. The musical hinterland of *thumri* was dominated by the Krishna cult and the associated rituals etc. Presentation and content of the *thumri* were thereby greatly influenced.

Structure

As in *khayal* (>), *thumri* has two parts: *sthayi* and *antara*. It is usully sung in *tala*s such as *deepchandi, roopak, addha, Punjabi*. They are characterized by a special lilt, absent in the *tala*s employed in *khayal*s.

Depending on the individual temperament of the artiste, thematic thrust and the kind of particular composition selected, three strategies of elaboration are followed in presenting a *thumri*, though in varying proportions. They are:

1   Distributing words in the rhythmic framework in order to create lilting patterns. This is known as *bol-bant*.

2   Evoking subtle shades of mood through combinations of words and melodic phrasings. This is known as *bol-banav*.

3   Using different non-verbal modalities interchangeably to express the same mood. This is achieved by creating emotion through gestures that approximate graceful dancing, and inversely falling back on words to evoke gesture-situations of dramatic significance. These two procedures are known as *bolme bat* and *batme bol*.

A *thumri* singer employing all or some of the strategies creates an impact entirely different from that of *khayal*s which often are similar to *thumri* in other structural features.

The last phase of *thumri*-singing usually sees the doubling of the tempo and greater scope for the *tabla*-player to weave rhythm-patterns characterized by sprightly presentation and delicate touch. These are known as *laggi*s. As popular etymology would have it, *laggi* is a shortened version of the Hindi phrase *'lag gai'* meaning 'it hits'! The singing in double the tempo is known as *dugun*. It seems that the last phase is not regarded mandatory by many performers.

Types

It may be safely stated that *thumri* can be classified according to the basic orientation it displays in favour of dance, *abhinaya* or music. Some types emerging from these performance-orientations are:

Lachau: Characterized by movements approximating dance.

Punjabi: Sung in the expansive *tala* of the name, it is a *khayal* but steeped in an evocative mood.

Bandishki thumri is sung in faster tempo, it has a greater word-density than other *thumri*s. Such *thumri*s are compositions in which syllabic units match rhythmic units in such a way as to create mutual rhythmic reinforcement. The contemporary *thumri*-singing has attained adequate maturity, variety of idiom, as well as repertoire to flower into different *gharana*s. Some easily identifiable *gharana*s are:

Gharana	Main features
Benaras	Dignified in gait, expansive in treatment, controlled in emotive utterance. Exhibits an approach of a *khayal*.
Lucknow	Decorative and explicit in expressing emotions. Closer to dance and shows affinity to *ghazal*.
Patiala	Flashy and yet highly moving. Less expansive and nearer to *tappa*.

Paradoxically *thumri*s are played on instruments such as *sitar*, violin etc. though the words and literary expressions are ruled out! It would be appropriate to describe the instrumental *thumris* as *dhuns*.

1.5.29 *Vishnupada*
A special variety of *dhrupada* (>). Saint-poet Surdas (1478-1583) brought *Vishnupada* into vogue and Mansinha Tomar (1486-1516) of Gwalher gave it royal encouragement. In the opinion of Abul Fazl (1551-1595-96) *Vishnupada* was characterized by a stanza of four to six lines and centred on the theme of the praise of Lord Krishna. *Tala* was selected according to the metre. Popularity of the *Vishnupada* was more or less confined to the religious centres and hence it does not seem to have enjoyed high concert profile.

1.6 Musical Forms (Instrumental)
It is not an exaggeration to say that a majority of instrumental musical forms in India are restricted to instruments of rhythm. This important orientation has some valid reasons:

Firstly, a number of instruments cannot but function as accompanying instruments. This is so because no instrument could be expected to develop a vocabulary, language and repertoire of its own unless it commands an innate capacity to produce a considerable variety of identifiable, typical and attractive individual sounds. Instruments lacking in this respect are many and they are automatically eliminated when instrumental musical forms are discussed.

Secondly, instruments capable of producing sustained sounds naturally turn to voice and vocal music to emulate the latter and concentrate on the melodic dimension. As a consequence, musical forms which they develop are modelled on the dominant forms of vocal music. These instruments have of course to clear the handicap of the unavailability of linguistic and literary resources which vocal music can explore and exploit so freely. However the greater tonal range and the marked variety of tonal colour together appear to provide an adequate compensation.

Thirdly, it is also noticed that instruments generally facilitate formation of unambiguously perceived rhythmic units, and individual instruments tend to evolve playing techniques particular to them.

In the final analysis, evolution of instrumental musical forms depends on the cumulative effect of all the three features referred to.

A reasonably correct guess could be made as to the relative antiquity or modernity of an instrument by examining the variety as also the multiplicity of forms it manages to develop. Other circumstances being equal, an older instrument could be expected to display an impressive array of forms because, by virtue of its long life, it gets time to grow and enjoy maturity of language and idiom.

A kind of 'survival of the fittest' principle also seems to prevail in music! If a new instrument proves capable of doing what an old one has been doing, and in the process guarantees a bonus of its own specific contribution, it tends to take over the musical forms already evolved. The older instrument is consequently forced to move back, however grudgingly!

Against this background it is not difficult to understand the reasons why major forms of instrumental music have evolved only in cases of *pakhawaj, tabla, been* and *sitar.*

What does traditional musicology tell us about instrumental musical forms? The medieval scene was extremely rich. Solo playing of instruments was described as *shushka* (dry)! Admittedly instrumental music-making not in accompaniment to dance or singing, was viewed condescendingly. Yet instruments enjoyed an abundance of musical forms. In respect of the medieval instrumental musical forms the following points are worth noting:

1   There were *vina*s of many types and they explored *raga*-music following in the steps of vocal music.
2   At least fifteen types of flutes existed. Flute-music too modelled itself on vocal music.
3   On the other hand rhythm instruments as a class presented a different picture as they *did* have their own forms of music. With reference to the membranophonic instruments the basic 'alphabet' of sounds producible (sixteen in case of *pataha* and thirty-two in case of the more developed *mridang*), prominent phrase-moulds resulting from them and forty-three resulting genres are discussed.
4   As is to be expected, separate genres for instruments of the idiophonic variety (*ghana*) are not described because such instruments are the least conducive to development of an independent repertoire.

This is the background against which the contemporary instrumental musical forms may be discussed.

1.6.1 *Bol* (v. H *bolna* = to speak)
Something which is said or uttered. A term of wide connotation with

varied applications in vocal and instrumental music. In the latter it is used at two levels:

At a lower level *bol* refers to all sound-syllables producible and useable in various ways to form meaningful arrangements during musical elaboration on all instruments except *pakhawaj*.

In *pakhawaj*-music however the term refers to a composition of sound-syllables which reflects faithfully the structure of a particular *tala*. Naturally it covers one full cycle and employs simple progressions.

1.6.2 *Chhed* (v. H *chhedna* = to begin, to initiate)

A phrase or a minor composition in *pakhawaj*-music customarily played or taught at the commencement of a solo concert or on the occasion of a disciple's initiation into *talim* (serious training under a *guru*).

1.6.3 *Dhun* (H < S *dhu* = to sound, to be agitated)

The term is used in the context of music made on melodic instruments capable of solo expression, e.g. *sitar, sarod, sarangi.*

It is a basic melodic framework with both *raga* and *tala* being treated as optional. As a genre in instrumental music a *dhun* fulfills the function of creating flexible and evocative moulds similar to those provided by *thumri, geet* or *bhajan* etc. in vocal music. As there is a comparative absence of grammatical restrictions in a *dhun*, a composer's imagination enjoys free play. Usually a *dhun* has two sections functioning as *sthayi* and *antara*. However a *mukhda* with some improvisations may also be described as a *dhun*. It is significant that as a rule *dhun*s are composed in non-major *raga*s or the *raga*s used in semi-classical forms of music.

1.6.4 *Gat* (H *gati* S *gam* = to go)

A term widely prevalent in instrumental music, its applications are notable in case of *tabla, pakhawaj, sitar, sarod* etc.

Pakhawaj

Some authorities hold that a *gat* has no place in the *pakhawaj*-repertoire. On the other hand some maintain that a composition without a *tihai* (>) and lasting for one cycle in *pakhawaj* music is a *gat*.

However another and an older tradition has it that a *gat* in *pakhawaj*-music actually refers to a specific *theka* (>) employed to provide accompaniment in the particular form of vocal music. For example a *khayalki gat* indicates *tala tilwada* which is abundantly used in *khayal*-singing. According to this tradition similar usages point to definite *theka*s employed to accompany *tappa, dadra, dhamar* and *ghazal*.

Tabla

In *tabla*-music *gat* constitutes a major compositional genre. Some important features of a *gat* are:

1 Generally it is speedy in movement.

2 It usually runs over many *tala*-cycles.

3 A *gat* enjoys a structure which does not follow strictly the segmentation of the *tala* concerned.

4 Compared to other genres a *gat* is remarkably rich in the degrees of sonority, and the syallabic density varies considerably. In addition the tempi are changed and no aesthetic strategy of treating the rhythmic material is left unexplored.

5 The compositional sections immediately preceding the *sam* often consist of 'weak' syllables in a *gat* in that it lends itself easily to successive repetitions.

6 Structurally a *gat* may or may not include *tihai*s and/or *rela*-passages to enhance the attractions of dynamics i.e. changes in volume and movement.

7 Unlike *peshkar* (>), *qayada* (>) etc. a *gat* is complete in itself and is not elaborated.

On account of their accomodative stance and flexible aesthetic policies *gat*s have become important indicators of a player's mastery over the instrument. In view of the great numbers and variety of *gat*s in circulation it is difficult to classify them exhaustively. Some important types are briefly described below:

a *Seedhi gat* (a. H straight, simple): In a four-four measure, the *gat* is first played in medium tempo amd immediately repeated in double tempo.

b *Rela gat*: A gat which includes a *rela* (>) in its final segment.

c *Manjhadhar gat:* (H a. in midstream) It is a *gat* characterized by highly unpredictable changes in tempi.

d *Tihai gat:* As suggested by the name it ends with a portion successively repeated thrice.

There are three sub-types:

i *Seedhi tihai:* simple.

ii *Akal tihai:* the beginnings of the *tihai*-sections remain unstressed.

iii   *Sab akal tihai*: all the stressable points (that is, the beginnings and the ends) of the *tihai* remain unstressed.

e   *Barabari* (equalized) *gat:* Characterized by medium tempo and even distribution throughout the composition.

f   *Tipalli gat:* Gat with its three successive sections set respectively in medium, one and a half and double tempo.

g   *Dumukhi gat*: *Gat* employing identical sound-clusters in the initial and final sections.

h   *Farad gat:* Gat discouragingly difficult in its initial and final section is called *farad* because it cannot be easily played successively. According to a tradition the composition invariably includes syllables *katta dhete kate tak dha* in the last segment, and these are to be played in double the tempo.

i   *Gat-paran:* It is claimed that the term is at least partially derivable from *parna* Skt. meaning a leaf. The related constructional pre and post-*khali* sections are identical.

j   *Jod/a gat:* (of a pair or couple, a double.) Composition inspired by an existing *gat* and very similar to it. Often it is also known as a *jawab* (answer).

k   *Gat-toda*: The composition borrows complexity of construction from the *gat* and flashy and attractive movement in the approach to *sam* from the *toda*s. However *gat-toda* is less ambitious in scope than a full-fledged *gat*. (See *tukada* for *toda*).

Sitar, sarod etc.

The major compositional genres in the music of *tata* (string) instruments which have attained concert stature are called *gat*s. In fact *sushira* (blown or wind) instrument such as *bansuri* or bowed string instruments (*sarangi*, violin) are also inclined to use *gat*s as the basis for their music-making. In solo music-making these instruments aim at *raga*-elaboration and hence need forms suitable for their individual technical resources. Unable to sustain the produced tones to any considerable length, *sitar* etc cannot hope to compete with *been* and other varieties of the *vina*. As a consequence the use of *dhrupad*, as a form to be exploited, is ruled out. Further, *sitar* etc. possess different timbre-personalities and cultural associations. For example, both *sitar* and *sarangi* had strong connections with music-making as practised by courtesans. The cumulative result led to an evolution of a sparkling and quick-stepped instrumental idiom and a determined effort to emulate *khayal* music. These were the circumstances under which *sitar* gradually emerged as a solo instrument in the last century and a half, evolving the *gats* in the process.

Sitar has developed two types of *gats* to achieve and to add to what *bada khayal* (>) and the *chhota khayal* (>) accomplish in vocal music. The two types are known as *Masitkhani* and *Razakhani* respectively.

Till about the middle of the nineteenth century a *sitar*-soloist relied on successive renderings of compositions of the type of *suravarta* (>) followed by those of precomposed *todas* (>). Performances of *sitar*-music were therefore short in duration and scope. The general tempo of music was from medium to fast, a feature inevitable in view of the nature of the instrument. Two corroborative facts need to be noted. To do justice to the improvisation and elaboration, it was a custom to play on *surbahar* before a switch-over was made to *sitar*. Secondly, *sitar* was in fact often regarded and described as a stepping stone for a student aspiring to graduate to *been* or other *vinas*. A number of factors changed the situation and enabled the *sitar* to nudge out the *been*s, the *surbahar*s and the *vinas*. Even though it is difficult to establish a clear chronology of events, their consequnces prove their logic.

1   Masitkhan thought of evolving a musical genre with an in-built provision for the slower musical statements and elaborations as in *khayal* with a greater scope for improvising techniques developed to maturity in vocal music as well as in the earlier string instruments.

2   To facilitate the sustained production of notes (so necessary to emulate voice and vocal music) more playing strings were added, increasing their number from three to five. This also led to a greater tonal range.

3   Masitkhan also arrived at a concept of a graver musical import and hence created a type of *gat* that deliberately eschewed the use of *chikari* (high-pitched side-strings) and the *taraf* (high-pitched sympathetic strings). Also ruled out was the employment of the comparatively flippant-sounding joint sound-syllables. In sum, the tempo, the vocabulary and the techniques were collectively harnessed to create music which is essentially continuous, serious and challenging.

Thus emerged the *Masitkhani gat* which has a *mukhda* (>) of the duration of about four beats. Usually set to *teentala* and played in slow tempo the improvisations and the *mukhda* of this *gat* are employed as in *khayal*. Accompanied by *tabla*, the *Masitkhani gat* has two sections functioning as *sthayi* and *antara*. Sometimes an intervening stanza is composed and it is aptly described as *manjha* (middle, intervening). There are obvious parallels to *khayal* even in the structure of the *Masitkhani gat*.

The *Masitkhani gat* is followed by one called *Razakhani*. The latter is a fast-paced composition set in a *raga* and a *tala*. This *gat* may begin from any beat and during the elaboration it generously uses *tihai*s, fast paced *todas* as well as the *jhala* (>). The Razakhani also has two sections called *sthayi* and *antara* and the similarity to the *drut khayal* in matters of structure and import are easily perceived. Very aptly the Razakhani gat has been described as *duguni gat* (a *gat* in double the tempo).

1.6.5 *Jhala* (H)

A term employed in different senses in the music-making of *pakhawaj*, *sitar, sarod* etc. It is only in case of *pakhawaj* that *jhala* refers to a form of music; hence it finds a place here. In the case of other instruments *jhala* is a particular technique of playing the instrument. It would therefore be discussed in their respective contexts at appropriate places.

In *pakhawaj*-music, *jhala* is a composition basically designed to provide accompaniment to the final and the faster phases of music made by string instruments.

The distinguishable structure of *jhala* has individual units of three, four or more beats. Due to the manageable duration of the individual units a *jhala* composition can be easily fitted into any particular *tala*. While rendering the *jhala* to match the elaboration on the string-instrument, the units are accentuated as required but care is taken to keep a continuous stream of units. It may be said that *jhala* is a rhythmic and membranophonic response to a musical stimulus-situation created by string instruments.

In *pakhawaj* the *jhala* which uses the sound-syllables in abundance is known as *kattar jhala*.

1.6.6 *Ladi* (H series, garland)

A form in *pakhawaj* music. It is a composition relying on close and repeated entwinements of sonorous sound-clusters such as *dhum kit tak tak* employed in various permutations and combinations.

In string-music (especially *sitar* etc.) *ladi* is a technique of binding together the tonal material.

A *ladi* composition in *pakhawaj* and *tabla* employing the syllabic structure *kattar* is known as *kattar ladi*.

1.6.7 *Lad-gutthi* (H *lad* + *gutthi* = knot)
Lad (>) with a sound-cluster designed to introduce a 'knot' within the compositon. For example, in a *ladi* of *dhumkit*, a cluster of *kda-dhan* would be introduced to momentarily arrest or 'entangle' the flow of the composition to create a complexity in the total pattern obtained. As a composition in *pakhawaj*-music, *lad-guthhi* represents a technique of organizing the tonal material in response to music in string instruments such as *sitar* etc.

1.6.8 *Lad-lapet* (H *lad* = series, garland + *lapet* = to wrap around)
Essentially a term indicating a playing technique in string instruments such as *sitar* etc. *Lad-lapet* presents a minor composition in membranophonic rhythm instruments. In *lad-lapet*, passages of the *lad* (>) type are interspersed with places wherein an effect of a *meend* (legato) is created by rubbing the skins of the drum-faces.

1.6.9 *Laggi* (v. H *lagana* = to use, to apply)
Essentially any attractive sound-patterns or syllables played in double tempo in *talas keharwa* (eight beats) and *dadra* (six beats). Conventionally *laggi* is employed to accompany the renderings of *thumri, dadra* and other similar semi-classical musical forms.

A reverberating use of the *bayan*, delicate though sharp tappings on the edges of the *tabla*-membrane, a skilful use of wrist-pressures, and the slight rubbings on the *bayan*-membrane and such other special effects are abundantly employed in the *laggi*.

1.6.10 *Mohra* (H *muha* S *mukha* = mouth)
A form in *tabla*-music. In one completed cycle of a *tala* if the last segment includes three *dha*-sounds, the variation is known as *mohra*. In fact a wider interpretation of the term suggests that any rhythmic, *tabla*-phrasing employing open sounds in a *mukhada* (>) used in accompaniment is known as *mohra*.

1.6.11 *Mukhada* (H S *mukh* = mouth)
A form in *tabla*-music. Similar to *tukada* (>) in intent and construction, *mukhada* however spans a longer duration of about eight beats. Usually a *mukhada* begins at *khali/kala* (>).

1.6.12 *Padar*
A term in *pakhawaj*-music (see *rela*). A composition which has a sound-

cluster for each of its beats. Some maintain that *padar* is derivable from *prastar* (S) which generally means an elaboration of phrase or an idea etc.

1.6.13 *Paran* (H S *parna* = leaf)

The most important form of composition in *pakhawaj*-repertoire. Some have suggested that *paran* is derived from the medieval *tala pooran* which was cluster of rhythmic, instrumental syllables employed to fill gaps in the structural points of a *tala*-frame.

From the various definitions some characteristics emerge strongly:

1   As a composition *paran* moves precisely in correspondence with the tempo of the *tala* concerned.
2   It employs sound clusters other than those used in the *tala* it is played in.
3   Both the open and the closed syllables of the *pakhawaj* are skilfully and flexibly woven in the *paran*.
4   A major compositional genre, *paran* unhesitatingly borrows formats from the repertoires and modalities of other instruments to enrich its own set of moulds. As a consequence it can boast of innumerable varieties warranting a major classificatory exercise if justice is to be done to its contribution to the *pakhawaj*-repertoire.
5   Usually *paran* needs two or more *tala*-cycles for a complete rendering.
6   A *paran* may or may not include a *tihai*.

Some of the major types of *paran*s and the criteria relevant to them are briefly described below:

a   The structural pauses within the composition are used in different ways and *paran*s are accordingly brought together in a class. For example:
     Bedam paran: Without pause. A *paran* with successive *tihai*- sections is called *bedam* while the one which allows a pause is known as *damdar* (with a pause).
     Atit: A *paran* which is completed one beat beyond the *sam* of a *tala*.
     Anagat: A *paran* which is completed one beat prior to the *sam* of a *tala*.
b   Association with a descriptive content distinguishes a class of *paran*.
     Chhavi paran: It draws a portrait of God with words which lend

easily to rhythmic arrangements analogous to sound-syllables particular to *pakhawaj*.

Madandahan paran etc. describe a mythological event in a language parallel to the *pakhawaj*-syllables arranged in rhythmic groupings.

The same criterion applies to *paran*s that are regarded auspicious because they are in praise of deities. For example *Ganesh paran, Maruti paran, Shiv paran, guru paran* are noteworthy.

Unless one wants to create another separate class, the *ashirwad* (blessings) and the *salami* (salutation) may also be considered descriptive and auspicious.

c   Affinity to a particular *tala* in which the *paran* is not played creates a type. For example *jhampangi paran* would be played in *adital* etc. but would be characterized by a progression that recalls *jhampatala*.

d   *Paran*s may be inspired by specific movements etc. of nonmusical origin and the rhythmic mapping may reflect the origin e.g. *jhoolna* (swing-movements), *kandukkrida* (playing with a ball)

e   Some *paran*s have a declared thematic and movemental dance orientation with appropriate names, e.g. *ras paran, maharas paran, nrittyangi paran, nachka paran*.

f   Some *paran*s are characterized by the special sound-effects they are designed to create. The sound-syllables are selected accordingly, prefatory legends are narrated fittingly and movements are executed precisely. The way some *paran*s of this class are composed, one is almost tempted to conclude that the concept of programme music is hardly alien to Hindustani music! For instance the following traditional *paran*s may be noted.

Karneka paran, tasheka paran, and *nagareka paran*: Respectively imitate the playing of *karna* (a type of horn), *tasha* (bowl-shaped small pair of drums used in processions) and *nagara* (a big drum employed in marching music).

Titodi paran: Onomatopoeic imitation of the calls etc. of the common Indian bird *titodi* (lapwing).

Hathiko rokna paran: The legendary *paran* that stopped an elephant in its tracks!

Hathiko nachana paran: The legendary *paran* that made an elephant dance!

Railki dhvani paran: An obvious rhythmic response to a modern situation, the *paran* onomatopoeically creates the dynamics of a railway engine steaming ahead.

Kadak bijli paran: Suggestive of 'thunder and lightening' effect.

Top ki paran: The event represented is the firing of a cannon.
What is remarkable is that a detailed presentation is attempted
and equally detailed directions are given. An assiduous attempt
is made to imitate the act of firing a cannon by closely following
the movements, rhythms and the sound-dynamics involved. For
example a break-up of the successive stages would reveal following parallels:

Action	*Meaning*
playing in the triple tempo	movement of the cannon wheels
playing in one and half times	cleaning the cannon-barrel with an iron-bar
— do —	initial explosion of gunpowder
playing in triple tempo.	the dying out of the explosion

g   Some *paran*s employ special playing techniques and their names
carry the suggestion.

Ek-hatti paran: To be played with one hand.

Du-hatti paran: To be played with both hands.

Tali-ki paran: That which has gaps to be filled with hand-claps.

Jai shabdaki paran: (*jai* = hail, victory): This composition includes utterance of word *jai*, while hitting the leather straps of
the instrument in addition to the normal playing on the
membranes.

h   Some *paran*s are inspired by other *paran*s already in existence
and as such allude to them. Hence they are described as *jawabi*
(answer) or *jodka* (in couple or a double).

i   Variation in tempi characterizes some *paran*s: hence they constitute a class by themselves. Examples are:

Ad paran: It is in one and half times the tempo of the *tala* concerned.

Gopuccha: The name (cow's tail) suggests a progressive thicken-
ing and tapering off. In rhythm this is translated in terms of the
tempi used. Beginning with a fast tempo the composition moves
to medium and then slow tempo and then to fast etc.

j   A very important class of *paran* is constituted by those featuring
some kind of structural complexity which also makes special
demands on the technical virtuosity of the player.

i)   *Bina-dha* or *bina-kiti paran*: Omitting certain important sound syllables throughout the composition is one way of composing a specially effective *paran*.

ii) *Tehttis-dha paran*: Going to the other extreme and using particular sound-syllables repeatedly makes interesting parans. One such is the *paran tehttis-dha* which includes the letter *dha* thirty-three times within one single composition!

iii) *Ulti paran:* As the name suggests the progression reverses itself to complete the composition in the manner of abcd-dcba.

iv) *Sundar-singar* (beautiful decoration): Compositions described as of this class are reputedly 'the complete' compositions because they include every important sound-syllable producible on *pakhawaj*. Such *paran*s are also regarded significant educationally and mastery over them is considered equivalent to mastery over the total range of the instrument.

v) *Jagahki paran* (place): The same composition is played in succession from the first, second etc. beat of a *tala*, thus resulting in special intricacy. Each new starting-point is described as *jagah*.

vi) *Farmaishi paran* (adj. H P *farmaish* = special polite request)

vii) *Kamal* (adj. H *ara* 'involving extreme skill).
According to a tradition the composition has three *dha* sounds in its *tihai* and none of them come on the *sam*.

k Some *paran*s are specially designed to provide accompaniment and are therefore known as *sath paran*. There are various ways in which meaningful words are employed in composing *paran*. For example:
Birudavali paran: It is composed of names, adjectives in praise of king, God etc. The praise-words often alternate with the sound-syllables of the instrument.
Sarthak paran: The composition uses meaningful words and sound- syllables of the instrument in such a way that though both appear alternately each forms a coherent sentence taken separately.

l Some *paran*s are minor in scope and intention thus nearly amounting to casual utterances as *chhutkar* or *chhutput paran*.

1.6.14 *Peshkar* (H *pesh* = to present respectfully)

A composition-type in solo-*tabla* corpus customarily presented at the commencement (as the first item) of the performance. Played in a perceptibly slow tempo, the *peshkar*, as a composition, is characterized by a balanced distribution of the sound-syllables produced on *bayan* (>)

and *dayan* (>) of the *tabla*. A *peshkar* is elaborated through various permutations and combinations of sound-syllables, tempi-variations etc. Employment of sound- syllables other than those in the composition presented is not prohibited in a *peshkar*, hence the choice is wide, unlike that in a *qayada* (>) In fact *peshkar*, it is often argued, is designed to allow the player to warm up by exploring the possibilities of the instrument and the player's form.

1.6.15 *Qayada* (H U = law)

An important composition-type in the solo *tabla*-repertoire. It is more structured than *peshkar* (>) and *qayada* is customarily played after the former. A *qayada* is characterized by its close relationship with the basic design of the *tala*. It is an arrangement of sound syllables of *tabla* set in a particular *tala* expected to be elaborated through permutations-combinations, tempi-changes etc. executed with the same sound-syllables as in the original *qayada*. Further a *qayada* is so structured that patterns and sound-syllables in *khali* (>) segment are matched by those used in the *bhari* (>) segment of the tala.

A *qayada* is elaborated in four well-defined phases appearing in sequence and known as *mukh, dora, bal* and *tihai* respectively. The first phase is *mukh* (mouth) in which an unelaborated and unadorned *qayada* is presented in equal time.

The second phase called *dora* (thread) divides the composition presented in the *mukh*-phase into smaller units to facilitate patterning during the elaboration.

Bal (twist), also called *palta* (reversal), constitutes the third phase. In it, patterns created out of the sound-syllables of *qayada* are rendered in close adherence to the structure of tala in which the *qayada* is composed.

The final phase employs *tihais* (>) to round off the elaborations of a particular *qayada*.

1.6.16 *Rela* (H)

A form in *pakhawaj* and *tabla* music.

Pakhawaj: From amongst the sound-syllables used in *sath* (>) composition, those which are conducive to renderings in four-fold or eight-fold tempo are woven into a coherent pattern called *rela*.

A special variety of the *rela* in *pakhawaj* is known as *pader*. More extensive than an ordinary *rela*, it employs sound-syllables of shorter duration and usually eschews the use of *tihai* (>).

Tabla: A *rela* in *tabla*-music is so structured as to consist of initial sonorous sound-syllables, followed by short medial sound-syllables and a consonantal final sound-syllable.

This constructional mode results into a near fusion of the successive sound-syllables to create an almost continuous sonar movement even though the rhythmic framework is not obliterated. All elaborations of a *rela* are rendered without allowing noticeable pauses because speed and near-consinuous stream of patterns constitute the essence of a *rela*.

1.6.17 *Sath* (H S *sahit* = with)

It is a form in *pakhawaj*-music. In other usages it means accompaniment. In the former context *sath* is a pattern of rhythmic sound-syllables running the full distance of a *tala*-cycle from *sam* to *sam*. It may or may not have *tihai*.

It is helpful to remember that a *sath* does not strictly follow the *tala*-pattern unlike a *theka* (>) as the former is more than a nominal variation of the *tala* concerned.

1.6.18 *Suravarta* (S *sur* = note + *avarta* = cycle)

A form in *sitar*-music. It is an introductory composition set in *raga* and *tala* for a *sitar*-solo. In the early phases of evolution of *sitar*-music a *suravarta* followed by *todas* (>) was the customary order of performance.

In addition to being a form of music, *suravarta* has educational significance. When not couched in sound-syllables of the *sitar*, *suravartas* become useful exercises or practice-lessons designed to provide a sound introduction to the *raga*-grammar. It could be said that this aspect of the *suravarta* and the *sargamgeet* (>) in vocal music are cognate musical entities.

1.6.19 *Talamala* (*tala* + *mala* = garland, series of *talas*)

An extended composition in *pakhawaj* music. Various *tala*-patterns are brought together in it successively to form one single pattern to be elaborated by using the usual strategies. *Talamalas* with a span of ninety to one hundred and forty beats in one cycle exist in the known traditional repertoires.

1.6.20 *Theka* (v. H *thekana* = to support)

An arrangement of sound-syllables employed in *pakhawaj*, *tabla* etc. designed to reflect the structural features of the *tala* concerned.

In *pakhawaj*-music especially, a *theka* may be described as a minor form played as a variation on the *tala*-pattern concerned. It traverṣes the entire cycle of the *tala* and one single *tala* might have many *thekas*. However a *theka* is not elaborated and as such it is not a generative rhythmic form.

1.6.21 *Tihai* (H S *tri* = three)

Any three-time repetition of a pattern of rhythmic sound-syllables is known as *tihai*. A *tihai* in which the two inbuilt terminations are followed by a pause is called *damdar tihai*, while a *tihai* without such pauses is called *bedam*.

A very important variety of the *tihai* mode of organizing rhythmic material is called *chakradar* (one with circle). Such a *tihai* contains smaller *tihai*s within each of its three sections making special demands on the composing as well as performing skills. According to some experts this type of *tihai* has been taken from the dance repertoire to be incorporated in *tabla* music.

Actions such as greeting, salutation etc. are woven into a performance of certain *tihai*s. They are therefore known as *salamiki tihai, namaskari tihai* etc.

1.6.22 *Toda* (H S *trut* = to cut away) *Tukada* (>)

A compositional format in *sitar*-music. A short piece made out of *sitar* sound-syllables such as *da, ra* and their various combinations and permutations is known as *toda*. In the early phase of the evolution of the instrument, *toda*s formed an important item in the repertoire. These highly pre-composed expressions do not allow improvisation.

1.6.23 *Tukada* (H S *trotak* = piece)

An attractive though a minor pattern of sound-syllables played prior to *sam* in *pakhawaj* and *tabla* music. Generally it covers a short span of two to four beats. A longer *tukada* may include a *tihai*.

A special variety of *tukada* in one and half times the tempo of the *tala* played is called *ad tukada*.

In *tabla*-music a *tukada* is also called *toda*. It is significant that *toda* also denotes a compositional format in dance (*kathak*). A *tukada* in *tabla* invariably ends with the sound-syllable *dha* (irrespective of the use of *dha* in the sam of the *tala*), a clear indication of its function to make immediate impact (*gat-toda* (>)).

2. Technical and Qualitative Terms

Term is a word that conveys ideas or concepts. Technical terms are words particular to a specialised field of knowledge. In the present context, names of instruments or their parts; *raga*s, *tala*s, musical forms and parts thereof; words pertaining to playing/singing techniques, styles and those referring to relationships between various muscial phenomena can be described as technical terms.

Technical terms form the warp and woof of all theoretical material on music. Misuse or misunderstanding of technical terms leads to inappropriate response to any musical situation.

Technical terms have certain characteristic features. Some of them are:

1   They are, realtively speaking, objective. They are outside the mind and do not vary from person to person.

2   An offshoot of their stability is their durability. The terms operate with the same or similar meanings for long periods and in the process prepare a strong basis for scholastic as contrasted with performing tradition.

3   Scholastic traditions are mainly expressed through codified technical terms which in the initial stages may or may not be written down. However, sooner or later the written mode gains an ascendancy. The entire apparatus relying on etymology, chronology, geneology, lexicography, construing, notation etc. assume important roles.

4   Technical terms often form clusters, because they deal with the same larger theme, namely music. However, the use of language and grammar also play an important role in the formation of clusters. Consequently a term originally coming into circulation as a verb may clear the way for related adverbs, adjectives etc.

5   Technical terms are units in the grammar of music; hence they
always remain a step behind the performing traditions. In other
words, actual concepts used in musical practice may have to wait
before they acquire a suitable technical term.

On the other hand qualitative terms are words that refer to the
value-aspect of things, events and processes. This aspect brings com-
parison into action. Hierarchies get established and subjectivity is
recognized as a legitimate tool for investigation into music. Actual performance and the performing tradition in which it is placed become
the prime movers. A quality-oriented concept is born in performance
and lives in it. However a concept may have to wait before it is verbalized even though it is in actual practice. A greater flux also characterizes the qualitative aspect as values and with them the correspond-
ing terminology change.

2.1 *Abhijata* (a. S of legitimate, acceptable birth)
A term used to indicate 'classical' as opposed to folk, primitive music
etc.

It obviously carries snobbish overtones not necessarily acceptable
to musicians. It is better to employ *shastrokta* (scientific) instead, indicating thereby the existence of codified rules. Further it is advisable
to use *shastriya* for music that exhibits a rule-structure which is not sys-
tematically codified.

2.2 *Achala* (a. S *a* = not + *chala* = moving)
The term lights up an interesting lexicographic field. Three related
and relevant meanings of *achala* are:
1   immovable, constant
2   seven
3   one name of the Indian cuckoo, is *achala tvish* (*tvish* = speech).

Achala swara: Notes which do not admit *komal*, *tivra* (flat, sharp)
states or degrees. *Sa* and *pa* (that is *shadja* and *panchama*) have been
regarded *achala* for the last four hundred years or so.

Achala that: In instrumental music it means a particular kind of arrangement of the frets in string instruments. An instrument with
separate frets for each of the notes is described as having an *achala*
that. Shifting or moving of frets is thus rendered unnecessary (e.g.
been).

Functionally, accompaniment has always been an important function of the fretted string instruments. With the solo vocalists shifting

keynotes at will to create shadows of *ragas* not directly being elaborated, the accompanying instrumentalists naturally faced technical difficulties (as frets could not be shifted repeatedly and immediately). The latter, therefore, established the *achala* that accommodating all notes in one octave.

A type of *vina* was called *achala* or equally aptly, *dhruva* (constant) in *Sangit Ratnakara and it was tuned to provide a constant reference.*

Achala is also known as *avikrit* (undistorted, unchanged). The antonym is *chala*.

2.3 *Acchop* (a. H S a = not + *chhup* = to conceal)

A rare *raga*, that is, one which is not in general circulation, is described as *acchop*. A more technical term of a similar import is *aprachalita*. *Raga*s befitting this description are complex in construction and movement. They often consist of phrases characteristic of various other *raga*s established in their own right. *Apoorva* (not before) is a synonym.

2.4 *Ad* (a. H S *ati* = something which can conceal or H *ad* = horizontal, oblong)

The term indicates an important mode of organizing rhythmic material.

The process of converting a four-four measure into one of four-three is *ada*. To convert a three-three measure into a three-two is called *kuad*.

The basic characteristic is that *ada* shifts all existing accents in a rhythmic pattern precisely in the middle of the existing accents.

2.5 *Adhama* (a. S = the lowest)

In Hindustani music three terms are used to indicate overall qualitative levels of the concerned phenomena. The terms are: *adhama* = the lowest, *madhyama* = the medium and *uttama* = the best.

With diminishing severity of tone they also indicate lower, medium and the top portions of the human body or those of the musical instruments.

The triad is additionally employed in respect of *raga*, *tala*, material of instruments, composers etc. thus evincing a wide application.

2.6 *Ahata* (a S struck, beaten)

The generic term describes all sound used in music. The other kind of sound namely *anahata* (not struck) is only perceived by *yogi*s.

2.7 *Alankara* (S *alam* + *kru* = to adorn, decorate, grace)
A very important concept with extensive aesthetic and musicological
implications is that of musical embellishment or *alankara*.

Basically *alankara* is a pattern resulting from various permutations
and combinations of different fundamental musical components.
Though it exists in both *raga* and *tala*-dimensions of Hindustani classical music, a more detailed statement about *alankara*s is available in
vocal music. As a consequence it is the melodic aspect which is more
prominently explored in the formulation of *alankara*s.

Two fundamental categories of *alankara*s are the *varna*-oriented
and the *shabda*-oriented. The former explore and exploit the sequence
of notes and the latter concentrate on the quality of intonation. The
*varnalankar*s explore four sequential modes:

sthayi	same, single note appears in a series of individual units
arohi	notes appear in ascending order
avarohi	notes appear in descending order.
sanchari	*appear in a mixture of all the three viz sthayi etc.*

Traditionally sixty-three *alankaras* of the *varna* category are listed.

In the *shabda*-oriented category it is obvious that infinite number of
*alankara*s are possible. The conventional listing of fifteen varieties of
*gamak*s is relevant in this context. Unfortunately all of them are not unambiguously identifiable.

Khatka, murki, behlava, meend and other *alankara*s are known and
employed today. They are discussed separately under appropriate
headings.

2.8 *Alapa* (S *alap* = narration, talk. *a* = near, towards, from, all sides,
all round + *lap* = to cause to talk, narrate)
A generic term which connotes elaboration of musical ideas, on the
melodic axis in or out of *raga*, with or without *tala*, in vocal or instrumental music. Elaborations on rhythmic dimensions would be
usually described by the term *vistara* (>).

In *alapa*, two features are generally important, the tempo and the
weightage given to various embellishments. In turn both are determined to a great extent by the form of music and the selected modality
(i.e. vocal, instrumental etc.) The *alapa*s are, therefore, found to vary
according to the form and modality of music. However some general
features can be noted:

Irrespective of the musical modality, *alapa*s proceed from slower to
faster tempi. Three kinds of tempi are generally distinguished, *vilam-*

bita (slow), *madhya* (medium) and *druta* (fast). No absolute standards are prescribed for them. *Vilambita* is stated to be half of the *madhya* and *druta* as the double of the latter. In instrumental music, especially in string-music, *alapa*s in particular tempi (with certain accompanying features) have special names. This is not so in vocal music.

In vocal music it is popular to connect *alapa* with the vowel 'a' and argue that *alapa*s have to employ vowel-sounds. The advocacy is strong in *khayal*-music and with some justification because the usage indicates 'a' to be the vowel employed to a great extent. However, exigencies of performance rather than musicological and etymological prescriptions are responsible. Not only that vowels in general allow sustained sound-production (which is an essential melodic requirement) but they also encourage quicker movement over the available pitch-ranges.

In reality vowels 'eat out' the breath! Hence *alapa*s in *dhrupada-dhamar* (and often in *khayal*-singing) rely on combinations of vowels and consonants. In *dhrupada-dhamar* renderings, *nom-tom* (i.e. *alapa*s realized through combining meaningless syllables and vowels such as *nom, tom, ri, da, na, tana* etc.) therefore, acquires a place. In *khayal*-singing the same strategy results into combining words of the composition with vowels. This is known as *bol-alapa*.

Sometimes a term such as *madhyalaya alapa* (medium tempo *alapa*) is used suggesting thereby that the term *alapa* in itself is not an indicator of a particular tempo. However *alapa* is to be mostly understood to have a slow tempo. In vocal music *alapa*s in *druta* tempo are often identified as *tan*s (which strictly speaking is a musicological mistake). This usage is yet another indicator of the association of the slow tempo with *alapa*s. (*Bol-alapa, bol-tan* etc. being special phases of *khayal*-singing are discussed separately).

Thumri (>), a major form of semi-art music evinces a different approach to musical elaboration though *bol*s play an important role in it. A detailed discussion of *thumri* is found in a separate entry.

In string-instruments (especially in the musics of *been, sitar* and analogous instruments) there exists a well-developed system of musical elaboration which, in all probability, evolved in close correspondence to the singing of *dhrupada* (>). The basic features are:

1 *Auchar* (S *utchar* = articulation): Initial rendering of notes sufficient for an unambiguous indication of the *raga*-identity.

2 *Bandhan* (S *bandhan* = binding): Short but emphatic phrases characteristic of the *raga*.

3 *Qaid* (A restraint, constraint): Elaboration in which one note is

given central importance.

4   *Vistar* (S *vi* + *stru* = to spread, to cover): The term indicates free
and uninhibited elaboration for which the preceding phases are
a preparation.

In *dhrupad*-music four kinds of *alapa*s are distinguished depending
on their overall use of embellishment and the tempi. The kinds are
described as *bani* (S *vani* = voices). They are:

a   *Gandhar*: austere; characterized by sustained and slow progressions.

b   *Dagar*: comparatively more decorative. Also employs more cross
rhythms.

c   *Nauhar*: abundance of embellishments to the point of dazzling
the listener into submission.

d   *Khandar*: heavily relies on *gamak*s.

It is obvious that the *bani*s cannot be expected to be more than broad
stylistic classifications. Interchange of their characteristics would be
detected in performances according to the tempo employed and the
musical temperament of the concerned artist.

A more systematic phasing of the *alapa*s is put forward in the context of string-music with a greater role allowed to the technical resources of the instruments concerned. In this context the following phases
are worth noting:

Vilambit alapa: Chiefly consists of slow-tempo, *tala*-less elaboration
of the *raga*. A *mukhada* (>) characteristic of the *raga* is introduced
after each completed statement of an idea. The tempo increases
gradually and more fret-work and *gamak*s appear on the scene, instead of sustained tonal lines and even patterns.

Jod: In double the tempo of the *vilambit* and succeeding it, is
jod(coupled)-phase of the *alapa*s. It is here that complicated fret-
work and fingering of high-pitched string used chiefly for the drone-
cum-rhythm function become prominent.

Jhala: The *chikari*-work comes to the fore. Sometimes a small *tukada*
(>) is also allowed an appearance. The increasing tempo registers a
movement towards musical climax. In this phase the entire musical
expression comes nearest to a metrical quality.

Thok: This post-*jhala* phase of elaboration is replete with accents. The plectrum etc. is actually struck on the adjacent wooden or metal portion of the instrument to introduce the *thok* (strike) effect.

Ladi: A phase confined to instrumental music. A nucleus of notes (and of sound-syllables in case of *pakhawaj* etc.) is formed and patterns are woven around the nucleus which is thus repeated in varied contexts.

Lad-gutthi: (a plait with a knot) A *ladi* with a 'knot'-effect created by introducing harder sound-syllables and their groups.

Lad-lapet: ladi-effect alternating with places in which *meend* and other enveloping sound-progressions are employed.

Paran: Patterns in string-music analogous to the accompanying *pakhawaj*-passages.

Sath: In it the string-player and the rhythm-accompanist proceed in strict correspondence.

Dhuya: Chikari-string is used for phrasing *ladi*s alternating with other patterns on the main strings.

Matha: In alternating movements *chikari* and the main strings are played upon.

2.9 *Amukta* (S not free, *a* = not + *mukta* = free)

Refers to a feature in the fingering technique of wind instruments such as *bansuri* (>). In it the sound-holes are completely blocked. *Mukta* (open) and *ardhamukta* (half-open) are the two other related varieties.

2.10 *Anga* (S division or department, a portion or part of a whole)

The gamut of the basic musical notes including the octave would consist of eight notes. It would thus become divisible in two halves of four notes each. The first half is called *poorvanga* (the prior or the previous *anga*) and the second half as *uttaranga* (the latter *anga*). The two *angas* are similar in construction and in the number of constituents.

One of the important characteristics of *raga* is that it has a pair of significant notes called *vadi* (>) and *samvadi* (>). It would be obvious that the pair is formed by taking a note each from the two *angas* to determine the member-notes of the pairs. Thus *sa-pa, re-dha, ga-ni* and *pa-sa* are the perfect consonances (that is arrangements realized through a note and its fifth) is evident in the formation of the pairs.

A sub-characteristic of *raga* is also derived from the *anga* concept. The *anga* in which *vadi* of a *raga* is located is regarded as important. *Anga-pradhanya* (importance of the *anga*) becomes therefore a guiding principle in performance. It also serves as a distinguishing mark in musicological descriptions.

2.11 *As* (H S *as* = to abide, to remain, continue to be in any state)
The persistence of sound after the cessation of its actual production. Often used to denote a continuous or uninterrupted action. Alternatively the term *as* is also derivable from *ansh* = part.

2.12 *Antarmarga* (S *antar* = internal + *marga* = path)
A very useful term which is unfortunately not in general circulation. It refers to the characteristic movement of notes within a particular *raga* indicating their abundant or limited use. For example, a note may be used but not repeatedly, or it may be slurred or stepped over. Such particular ways of using the notes are known as *anabhyasa* and *langhana*, respectively. *Vadi* ($>$) a note being used repeatedly by definition, is kept out of the purview of these terms.

Thus *antarmarga*s are expressed through *alpatva* (scarce use) *and bahutva* (abundant use). The former is realized through *anabhyasa* (a single time use) and *langhana* (stepping over). For the latter (that is, *bahutva*), *abhyasa* (repetition) is the royal road.

2.13 *At* (H *at* = obstacle, objection; S *atani* = that end of the bow which has a niche to tie the bow string)
The strip located before the first fret of *sitar* etc. to provide a supporting niche to the string passing over to the peg.

2.14 *Avanaddha* (adj. S *avanaddha* = covered; a common term for membrane-covered instruments of rhythm broadly described as drums)
According to the usage in Pali literature *avanaddha* instruments were described, rather confusingly, as *vitata*. Another minority tradition subscribed to the view that rubbed *avanaddha* instruments are to be described as *vitata*. However, as argued by Pandit Lalmani Mishra, *avanaddha* instruments with strings (to which the term *vitata* has a direct reference) are better described as *tatanaddha*.

Anaddha is an alternative term.

A large number of *avanaddha* instruments operate in various musical categories. The individual instruments necessitate separate descriptions for fuller appreciation of their distinctive identities and special contributions. However some important structural features commonly found in *avanaddha* instruments can be noted:

Mukh: (S *mukha* = mouth) the face of a drum covered by membrane

Khod/ar: (H *kotar* = hollowed trunk of a tree from which the body of an *avanaddha* instrument is made

Bhanda: (H S *bhand* = body of an avanaddha instrument made of metal)

Patal: (S membrane)

Pudi: (H membrane)

Gajra: (H *ganj* = group) A plait of leather or thin rope holding the membrane evenly stretched over the face

Rassi/dori: (H) Small rope of leather or cloth used to stretch the membrane. Leather strips that perform a similar function are called *baddi*

Ghera/kada: (H) A metal ring around which a leather plait is woven

Gatta: (H) Wooden blocks inserted under the *rassi* to tighten the latter and increase the tension on the membrane

Ghar: (H S *griha* = house) Section of a *gajra* formed by a *rassi* passing through it. Stroking the sections upwards reduces the tension on the *pudi* and decreases the pitch. A downward stroke has the opposite effect.

Masala/siyahi (H P *syaha* = blackness) A thin circular coating of iron filings, carbon, boiled rice etc. applied on membranes to improve their timbre

Chhalla: (H S *challi* = creeper) Small brass rings passed through *rassi*s to tighten or loosen the *rassi*s and hence the membrane, in order to heighten or lower the pitch

Gittak: (H) small piece of metal, wood etc

Kinar: (P *kinarah*) edge of a strip, membrane etc

Ghundi: (H S *guntha*) button-shaped knot of cloth, rope etc.)

Shanku: S a cone-shaped solid body

Indavi: a ring of cloth to keep/rest an instrument

Lav: minuscule hair, wool on animal skins etc. used to prepare membranes

Dhancha: skeleton

Dandi/danda: bar

Penda/pendi: base
Chabi: key screw
Ghat/ghada: clay-pot
Lakdi: wooden stick
Poolika: circular coating of paste
Jhanj: metal disk
Jhilli: a thin coating, covering
Udar pattika: strap going over a player's stomach to hold an instrument
Skandh pattika: strap going over a player's shoulder to hold an instrument
Chaddar: metal sheet
Khapacchi: a thin strip of bamboo, wood etc.

2.15 *Avartana* (turning round, revolution)
A complete cycle of a prosodic or rhythmic pattern. The concept is of special importance as the phenomenon of *tala* depends on circularity of the temporal progression. The term is also applied rather loosely to indicate repetitions.

2.16 *Badhat* (H *badhana* = to increase S *vardhana* = increase)
1   To move from slow to fast tempo.
2   Elaboration of *raga*s according to the established norms by stressing qualities of gradualness and attention to detail. A concern to project a larger musical pattern is also evident.

2.17 *Barabar* (adj. H P *var* = equal)
In tempo, a relationship of correspondence between units of song etc. and the accompanying rhythms.

2.18 *Bahutva* (S abundance, plenty)
In particular *raga*s some definite notes are used oftener than some others. The significance of notes in abundant use is indicated by the term *bahutva*. The antonym is *alpatva*. (see *antarmarga*)

2.19 *Baj* (H *baja* S vadya = mode of playing)
1   Style. The term is used in connection with certain forms (e.g. *dhrupada, khayal*) or with instruments (e.g. *mridanga*)
2   Also denotes a string in musical instruments, chiefly used to make music. For example the first string in *sitar* etc. is used for produc-

ing notes or effects in musical elaboration: it is described as *baj ki tar.*

2.20 *Bant* (v. H *bantna* = to distribute)
Distribution. An important procedure adopted in musical elaboration. Components of a musical composition are redistributed by varying their rhythmic, tonal and timbre-contexts to introduce novelty.

2.21 *Bemancha*
A term in *pakhawaj/tabla*-music. In case a performer foresees an overshooting of the *sam* (while completing a paran-composition etc.) he is allowed to improvise and add a *tihai* etc. to the composition to reach the next *sam*. The procedure is called *bemancha*. Etymology unknown.

2.22 *Chalan* (H S *chal* = to move)
A characteristic way or movement of organizing tonal/rhythmic material in musical manifestations of all kinds. A very inclusive term, *chalan* may allude to grammatical peculiarities of rhythmic/tonal groupings or changes introduced in them out of stylistic considerations.

23 *Chal* (H S *char* = gait movement)
Style in a narrower sense. Today it also means 'tune'. In the context of older poetic compositions, the term indicated a change in metre, and with it in tune.
Tarz, chalan are synonyms.

2.24 *Chapak* (v. H *chipakana* = to glue, to move closer)
A special way of producing sounds by striking left-hand fingers on the edges of the bass (left-hand) drum in *pakhawaj* and *tabla-* music.

2.25 *Chhanda* (H S to please)
Even though the term primarily connotes a characteristic of poetry it has contributed to the evolution of the concept of *tala*.
A unique feature of the Indian *chhanda*s is their invariable assocation with definite tunes. The tunes, being tonal moulds, raise the performance of *chhanda*s much above a simple *pathan* (recitation).

2.26 *Chhoot* (S *syoot* = sewn, stitched)
An important melodic embellishment which involves intonation of a

note or a cluster of them in successive octaves without touching the intervening notes.

2.27 *Darja* (H A *darj* = prestige, designation)

Term employed to indicate subtler distinctions in notes and rhythms. For example, *chadha ma* (heightened *ma* note) or *druta madhyalaya* (fast-medium tempo) are *darjas*. It is clear that *darja is* demonstrable rather than explainable. The usage of *darja* is more or less confined to the performing tradition.

2.28 *Deshi* (adj. S regional)

Roughly translatable as regional. Musicologically, *deshi* as contrasted with *margi* has been described 'as less governed (or at least more flexibly governed) by rules pertaining to *raga* and *tala,* comparatively recent in origin, preferred by the common people and changing according to the region of its origin.'

One may use the term today to describe folk music in India.

2.29 *Dhakit* and *dhumkit baj*

The two terms taken together describe aptly and fundamentally the overall style of *pakhawaj*-music. Firstly, they indicate a preponderance of the particular sound-syllables, namely, *dhakit* and *dhumkit.* Secondly, they serve as indications of patterning based on three or four units respectively as well as the sonorous timbre created by the clusters. The former is also described as *kattak baj* following a similar logic of relying on duration, pattern and sonority as criteria to describe the style *(baj)* of playing.

2.30 *Dhruvaka* (S *dhru* = invariable, stable)

In stanzas of compositions, line/s that recur at the conclusion of every stanza.

Palavapada is a synonym.

2.31 *Druta* (adv. S fast)

Indian music and musicology do not subscribe to the principle of absolute time. Hence *druta* is described as double of the medium which in turn is described as double of the slow *(vilambita)* tempo.

2.32 *Gamaka* (H S *gam* = to go, one who is going/moving)

A very accommodative term indicating a group of melodic embellishments in vocal and/or instrumental music. The core meaning of *gamaka* indicates a contextual use of a note, that is, providing it with a touch of the preceeding and/or succeeding note/s. Traditionally, *gamaka* is described as a vibratory effect in producing a tone to the delight of listeners.

The medieval *Ratnakara* tradition refers to fifteen varieties of *gamaka*s, the later Sangit Parijat to twenty, and some later performing traditions claim twenty-two types of *gamaka*s! Unfortunately the typology is not clearly explained.

The *gamaka*s can be classified according to duration required, range of notes covered and the special effect produced. One may also distinguish between vocal and instrumental *gamaka*s.

Some of the interesting and identifiable *gamaka*s are:

- *Tirip:* four notes in a short beat, producing in the process an effect of a *damaru* (a folk membranophone).
- *Tribhinna:* uses notes in a vibratory manner in three successive octaves.
- *Ahata:* uses an accent on the next that is the higher note.
- *Gumphit:* uses the 'hum'-sound.
- *Mudrita:* singing with a close mouth.

It is interesting to note that the word *gamaka* in Hindi also means fragrance. The embellishment surely adds to the beauty of music!

2.33 *Gana* (S singing)

A very basic and generic term. *Gana* refers to that linguistic/syllabic composition which provides a base for elaborating a *raga* or a *swara*.

The two main divisions of *gana* are known as *nibaddha* (bound, tied, fettered, stopped, closed, formed of) and its opposite *anibaddha* respectively. *Nibaddha gana* consists of five compositional sections *(dhatus)*; and it is set in *tala*. The *dhatu*s are:

1   *udgraha* = initial section
2   *melapaka* = section intervening between the first and the third
3   *dhruva* = section regarded mandatory
4   *abhoga* = section which completes the piece
5   *antara* = section optionally placed between third and fourth sections

2.34 *Ghana* (S compact, hard)

Perhaps the most thickly populated of the instrumental categories, *ghana* is described traditionally as 'that made of bronze'. Thereby solidity is suggested as the chief characteristic.

This variety of instruments had a very significant role to play during the medieval period. However, their circulation has been mainly restricted today to folk music. Some important structural features of these instruments are:

- *Dand/danda:* a bar to hold and lift the heavier of the *ghana* instruments.
- *Dolak/lolak:* a clapper inside bells etc.
- *Ankada:* a hook to hold the clapper.
- *Hathoudi:* hammer.
- *Nabhi:* navel, centre.
- *Chhalla:* a small metal ring.
- *Chaukhat:* frame.
- *Tukda:* piece of wood.
- *Patti:* strip of wood.
- *Ghundi :* a button-shaped knot of cloth, rope etc.
- *Gol* (ref. *ghungroo):* sphere-shaped metal body.
- *Goli* (ref. *ghungroo):* pebble-like small objects.
- *Dori:* rope.

2.35 *Gharana* (H *ghar* S *griha* = family)

Performing arts have been carried on as family traditions in a majority of cases. This has been so at least till the very recent past. The term *gharana* is therefore more appropriate in performing arts than in other arts. However, today the term has come to connote a comprehensive musico-aesthetic ideology changing from *gharana* to *gharana*.

At one point of time *gharana*s were understood to be indications of the place of origin of hereditary performing musicians. Hence the use of place names was regarded inevitable while describing *gharana*s. For example following are the names of *gharana*s in *khayal*: Agra, Gwalher, Patiyala, Kirana, Indore, Mewat, Sahaswan, Bhendibazar, Jaipur, Bishnupur etc.

As hereditary musicianship is not confmed to vocalists, *gharana* names also occur in instrumental contexts. For example in *tabla-* music we have Delhi, Ajrada, Farokabad, Punjab, Banaras etc. It is interesting to note that *gharana*s in *pakhawaj,* an instrument established earlier than the *tabla,* are person-oriented viz. Kudosingh, Panse etc.

Dhrupada-singing has *gharana*s but the names have been chiefly described in terms of musical and stylistic characteristics (see *dhrupada*).

Another important point has been the prominence of the concept during the nineteenth century. It has been plausibly argued that deprived of the munificent royal patronage after the advent of British rule, hereditary musicians were compelled to move to urban centres. In cities they stuck to the place-names of *gharana*s in an attempt to preserve their respective musical and regional identities.

However, during the modern period *gharana*s are being interpreted on the basis of their explicit or implicit musical ideologies. In the process, the regional or familial explanations are replaced. Persons with no musical background began taking to music seriously during the modern age. Affiliations are, therefore, formed on ideological basis today. This is also true in respect of *gharana*s in musical forms that have a recent history such as the *thumri* (>). The more mature the form or the instrument etc., the more the possibility of emergence of a *gharana*. This is the reason why there is a possibility today to have *gharana*s in *sitar* or *ghazal* etc.

Even today *gharana*s are discussed, proclaimed and justified with much passion, heat and pride! However it is clear that new musical alignments are taking place. In face of the media-explosion leading to easy accessibility to all kinds of music the validity and utility of the *gharana* is strongly questioned. It is up to musicians to reinforce the aesthetic basis of the *gharana*s if the concept is to contribute meaningfully to musical activity.

2.36 *Ghasit* (H *ghasitna* S *ghrisht* = rubbed, dragged)
A melodic embellishment prominently used in string instruments. Connotes a playing technique in which a note is produced through rubbing a string.

2.37 *Graha* (H S *graha* = to receive)
The core-meaning is 'to take or grapple or join with'.

Earlier *graha swara* indicated a note with which a *raga* was introduced. Later, when music became more *anibaddha,* that is free or improvised, rules regarding *graha swara* were observed with less rigidity.

Today the term indicates ways in which song/singing etc. and rhythm come together. Thus:
- *Sama* (equal) *graha:* Both commencing on the same beat.
- *Anagata* (not arrived) *graha:* Rhythm commencing before the singing etc.
- *Atita* (beyond) *graha:* Rhythm commencing after the singing etc.

2.38 Guna (H S quality, merit)
An acoustic term indicating quality of sound as contrasted with the other two dimensions namely pitch and intensity.

Traditional *guna* also means merits of artistes, instruments etc. For example *Naradiya Shiksha* (c. 500 A.D.), the earliest musicological text, refers to *dash guna*s (ten merits) of a singer.

2.39 *Guru*
1   Guide, preceptor or teacher (when used as a noun).
2   Units of long duration in prosody and music (when used as an adjective).

2.40 *Jamjama* (U to employ notes)
Reportedly, the melodic musical embellishment uses pairs of notes in perceptibly fast tempo, repeatedly and successively.

2.41 *Jarab* (A stroke)
In melodic instrumental music the basic 'up'/'down' strokes of the plectrum etc. are called *jarab*. These are associated with onomatopoeic sound-syllables.

2.42 *Jawab* (A answer)
The term has a larger, as also a narrower application. The former refers to any composition, part of it or a melodic/rhythmic phrase alluding to or suggestive of another part etc. within the same performance of music through the positioning, structural similarity or characteristic of the units concerned.

In a narrower sense *jawab* suggests relationship between notes distanced by four/five intervals.

2.43 *Jawari (sawari?)* (H S *jawa* = speed)
The term indicates a special effect of sound. A lingering, rounded sound, a resonance added to the sound of the original plucked/strummed sound of strings is called *jawari*.

In string-instruments strings pass over a bridge. The effect described as *jawari* is created by inserting a thread between strings and the bridge and strumming the string.

It is reported that in *tabla* a thread is inserted between the tensed membrane and the leather strip pasted over it at the edge to create a similar effect. Some harmonium manufacturers also refer to the term *jawari.* Voices are often described as voices with or without *jawari.*

It appears, that from the specific usage in relation to string instruments, the term and its connotation have spread over other modes of music-making to describe similar sound effects.

Jiwa is a synonymous term.

2.44 *Jhatka* (H *jhatakna* S *jhatta* = sudden shake or pull)
A melodic embellishment consisting of a fast movement from one note to another, with a stress on the latter note.

2.45 *Jila,* (A shine or *jil* = region)
A term indicating departure from the *raga* mentioned e.g. *jila Kafi.*

2.46 *Jod-nawaz* (H *jod* S *jud* = to join + *nawaz* P favour)
A person proficient in the *jod* phase of *alapa* (>) in elaboration of a *raga.*

2.47 *Kaku* (S tonal changes introduced to signify musical content)
In the context of dramaturgy the term meant 'change of voice under different emotions such as fear, grief, anger etc.' Its specific application to music led to a different typology. *Kaku* is described as producible from chest, head and neck respectively.

2.48 *Kampana* (H S *kamp* = to vibrate, tremble)
An important class of melodic embellishment in which a note is produced in such a manner that the entire range between the preceeding and the succeeding notes is suggested.

2.49 *Kana* (S *kan* = to go small or n (as a noun) = grain, particle)
Melodic embellishment in which a higher or a lower note is attached with a very light touch to the main note. The attached note is called a *kana swara.*

2.50 *Kanthadhvani* (H S *kantha* = throat + *dhvani* = sound)
The sound of voice. The medieval musicological statements on merits and demerits of voice were rich and thorough. In fact the tradition took a step further and traced particular voice qualities to specific states of human organism in terms of three basic humours namely *kapha* (phlegm), *pitta* (bile) and *vata* (wind) as propounded in *Ayurveda,* the Indian science of longevity.

However the basic distinctions made today in respect of *kan-thadhvani* are few. They are also loosely employed and vaguely under-stood. Three terms used with general agreement and in alignment with three acoustic parameters of pitch, volume and timbre need to be noted. They are: *uccha* (high pitched), *gambhira* (voluminous) and *madhura* (sweet). Antonyms are *dhali* (bass), *patli* (thin) and *karkasha* (harsh). Three other terms usually employed to describe subtler voice-qualities are: *halki* (quick in movement), *bhari* (slow in movement) and *jhardar/jawaridar* (resonant).

2.51 *Kharaj* (H S *shadja* = derived from six organs)
Indicates the bass octave. A special method of cultivating voice by practicing singing in the lower octave is known as *kharaj sadhana*.

2.52 *Khatka* (H *khatakna* = to create a sharp clashing sound)
A melodic embellishment in which a cluster of notes is produced fast and forcefully prior to the note projected as important.
    According to some, two synonymous terms are *gittakadi* and *murki*. A minority holds that *khatka* is a *gamaka* (>) which has two com-ponent notes.

2.53 *Khula-band* (H *kholna* = to open + *bandh* = tie, close)
Terms generally applied to ways of singing/playing describable as open *(khula)* and closed *(band)*.

2.54 *Krama* (S sequence)
Indicates sequence of musical notes in an ascending order.

2.55 *Krintana* (S)
An important playing technique in string-music. The forefinger of the left hand touches the fret lightly while the middle finger stretches the string out.

2.56 *Laghu* (H S short)
An important unit of measuring musical time. When the time re-quired for pronouncing of a letter is equivalent to the batting of an eyelid it is described as a *laghu*. It is also known as *ekamatrika*, that is, of one beat. However the minimal time-unit prescribed to be used in ancient *(margi)* music is five *laghus*. Significantly *deshi* (regional) music is stated to deviate from this requirement.

2.57 *Lakshana* (H S a mark, token, characteristic)
A general term used to indicate identifiable qualities of musical phenomena such as *raga, tala, gana.* Traditional statements of *lakshana*s are unfailingly perceptive and detailed.

In contemporary practice *lakshana* is used as a near-synonym of aptitude. Veteran *gurus* or performers use the term to indicate a disciple's or a young/new performer's potential.

While *lakshana* refers to a quality realizable in future, a *guna* indicates quality already achieved.

Derived terms are:

lakshanakara = An authority on musicology.

lakshana geet = (>)

lakshana grantha = A work on musicology.

lakshana-lakshaya-grantha = A work consisting of theory as well as compositions in actual practice.

2.58 *Lakshya* (H S *laksha* = to perceive, to define)
A classic work, composition etc. which belongs to the performing tradition as opposed to the scholastic. It is in other words an effort of a representative character presenting authentic renderings of *raga, tala* etc.

2.59 *Langhana* (H S *langh* = to jump over, to cross over)
An act of going 'over' a note without touching it or only slightly touching it. The technique helps in defining the character of a particular *raga* which, in the final analysis depends for its identity on the particular emphasis on notes, its chief components.

2.60 *Laya* (S *lay* = to move, to go)
Regulated motion is *laya*. The duration of rest between two strokes determining the duration of a *matra* is *laya*.

It is of three types: *vilambita* (slow), *madhya* (medium) and *druta* (fast). *Madhyalaya* provides the reference to determine the other two; and matra determines the *madhyalaya*. *Drutalaya* is double the *madhya*, and *vilambitalaya*, the half of *madhya*.

The two major applications of *laya* are in metrics and music. Both the applications interact with each other. While time-measurement in poetry employed the triad of *laghu, guru* and *pluta*, that in music ultimately settled on the trinity of *vilambita, madhya* and *druta*.

A related concept is *laya khanda*. It is a segmentation of a continuous movement through a grouping of strong-weak accents.

2.61 *Layakari* (H S *lay* + *kari* = to work on rhythms)
Introduction of rhythmic variations with reference to the assumed *laya;* also described as *alankarik* (decorative) *laya*. Five important varieties of *layakari* are stated as:

> *chatusra* = four in one matra
> *tisra* = three in one matra
> *khanda* = five in one matra
> *misra* = seven in one matra
> *sankirna* = nine in one matra

2.62 *Lopya/lupta* (H S *lup* = to cause to disappear)
A note omitted or to be omitted from a particular *raga*.

2.63 *Madhya* (H S middle)
An important term indicating a reference-state to help comprehend the relative highness and lowness in matters of pitch, and slowness and fastness in matters of tempo. The concepts of *mandra* (bass) and *tara* (treble), *vilambita* (slow) and *druta* (fast) are established in relation to the *madhya*.

2.64 *Manjha* (*madhya* = middle)
A section located between *sthayi* (>) and *antara* (>) is called *manjha* in compositions for melodic instruments. Such middle-units are also traceable in some *khayal* (>) compositions.

2.65 *Margasangeet* (S)
Ancient music aimed at offering devotion to God and performed in strict adherence to rules. Music-making contrastive to *margasangeet* in character was described as *deshi* (>). Also known as *margisangeet;* *margasangeet* does not claim today an identifiable separate corpus.

2.66 *Mata* (H S doctrine, tenet)
Opinion. Indian musicology attempted to classify the evergrowing number of *raga*s. A very early formula was codification of *raga*s into *raga-ragini-putra-vadhu* families. The approach was crystallized in various codifications known as *mata*s.

The prominent of the *mata*s were *Hanuman mata, Shiva mata, Naga mata*. Today the *mata*s enjoy merely an academic significance.

2.67 *Matra* (H S measure)
The basic unit of measuring musical time in general and *tala* in particular. Different opinions are expressed in respect of the precise time-value of a *matra*. For example,

a time required to pronounce five *laghu* letters.
b time required to bat an eye-lid.
c time required to pronounce one letter.

The concept of *matra* is also employed to define two values with longer durations namely *guru and pluta. Guru* is the time required to pronounce ten *laghus,* and *pluta,* fifteen *laghus.*

2.68 *Matu* (H S)
A useful general term for the language-component in musical compositions. The tonal component is described as *dhatu.*

2.69 *Misal* (*misil* A *misla)*
A term in *pakhawaj*-music; refers to the sequence in which various compositions are to be played in a solo performance.

2.70 *Meend* (H S *meedam)*
An important melodic embellishment in which the passage from one note to the lower is achieved by maintaining a continuity.

Musicological texts have dealt with the concept precisely in describing *meend* as a *karshankriya* (an act of stretching) to be further subdivided into four as shown below:

- *anagat meend* terminating before the desired note is reached
- *atikrant meend* terminating beyond the desired note
- *vicchhinna meend* breaking in between
- *vishamahata meend* displaying unevenness of strokes; hence temporal unevenness in the effect of continuity.

Even though the terms betray chordophonic bias the phenomenon also characterizes vocal music.

2.71 *Mela* (H S meeting, union, assembly)
The generative scale formulated through a sequential ascending and descending arrangement of eight notes from the fundamental to its octave.

Vidyaranyaswami of the Vijayanagara empire (estd. 1336) was the first user of the term. The later terms *sansthan, that,* as well as the Persian *mukam* are synonyms.

2.72 *Melakarta* (H S *mela* + *karta*)
A generative scale of seven notes arranged sequentially in their ascending and descending orders. Basing his formulations on a total number of twelve notes placed in one octave, Venkatmakhi advocated seventy-two *melakarta* scales.

2.73 *Mishra* (H S mixed, blended, combined)
A term used to classify sound, *raga* and many other constituents of Hindustani music.
    For example:
    Mishra-nada Sound produced by human breath and instrument
    Mishra-raga Resulting from a combination of two or more *raga*s
    Mishra-tala Combining two or more basic *tala*s
    Mishra-swara The sharp/flat states of the fundamental seven notes in the scale

2.74 *Mudra* (H S face, stamp)
Certain informational material is included in musical compositions through a feature called *mudra*. It usually occurs in the last line. Though *mudra* does not find a place in all forms of music it is however found in musics of art, devotional and some folk categories. Twenty-one types of *mudras* are noted though all of them are not present in each case. Thus *mudras* may include:

    i   name of a composer
    ii   pen-name of a composer
    iii name of a *raga/tala*
    iv   name of a patron
    v   name of a *guru*
    vi   name of a hero

2.75 *Mukha* (S mouth)
A recurring portion of a melodic composition occuring prior to the *sam*. It virtually acts as a clue to identify the composition. In addition, it fulfills the aesthetic function of providing a constant reference for variations introduced by the performer from time to time. *Mukhda* is a diminutive of *mukha*.
    The term is also employed to describe constructional parts of instruments especially of the aerophonic *(sushira)* and membranophonic *(avanaddha)* categories.

2.76 *Mukhari* (H S *mukh* = mouth)
A person knowledgeable enough to compose, recite and teach the rhythmic compositions used in dance. A *mukhari* controls the singer, rhythm-accompanist as well as the dancer in a dance performance.

2.77 *Murchhana* (S)
A sequential arrangement of seven notes in ascent and descent beginning every time with a different note. The western concept of modulation comes nearest to *murchhana.*

Application of the *murchhana* principle allows a significant contribution to patterning.

2.78 *Nada* (S)
Generic term for the concept of sound as a basic element of music both as an art and science. The fact that *nada* is regarded as basic to *Yoga* suggests an intrinsic relationship in Indian culture between music and *Yoga.* 'Na' is stated to symbolize *prana,* that is breath and '*da*' is fire. The two basic varieties of *nada* are *ahata,* that is produced through 'striking'; and *anahata,* that is produced without recourse to the process of striking. The former is used in music.

Subdivisions of musical nada are *anudatta* or *mandra* (base), *swarita* or *madhya* (middle) and *udatta* or *taru* (high). The basic principle applied to determine the relative highness/lowness holds that later the variety, double the pitch and vice versa.It is therefore clear that Indian musicology does not accept the principle of absolute pitch.

Many other classifications of nada are possible. For example Matanga in *Brihaddeshi* (800 A.D.) suggests:

sukshma = subtle
ati sukshma = very subtle
apushta = not filled/not full
pushta = full
kritrim = artifitial
The major synonyms are: *dhvani, rava, swana, kolahala.*

2.79 *Nara* (S man, male)
Bass tonal quality in instruments such as *pakhawaj,* harmonium etc. *madi* (P *Madah*) suggests the opposite quality.

2.80 *Nibaddh*a (S bound, fettered)
The fundamental musical characteristic of being rigorously regulated

by rules especially those pertaining to *tala*, chhanda, *yati* etc. is indicated by the term *nibaddha*. A contrastive tendency of being free of such constraints is suggested by the term *anibaddha*. Also see *gana*.

2.81 *Nikas* (H S *nishkasa* = to produce)

Production of sound syllables in instrumental music relevant to particular instruments. The term clearly refers to playing techniques in *pakhawaj, vina, sitar* etc.

In most cases the actual sounds produced by the instruments are roughly indicated by the 'alphabets' of the 'language' of the instrument. Hence a change in the *nikas* of a particular sound-cluster may actually bring about a considerable change in the final impact achieved. Therefore, *nikas* is of primary importance in performing traditions. To a great extent, *gharanas* are a result of developing, following and advocating particular techniques in *nikas*.

2.82 *Nikharaja* (H S *ni* + *kharaj shadja*)

Description indicating a highly diminished presence of *shadja* (*sa*, the fundamental) in a *raga*. In veiw of the overall importance of the principle of tonality, the feature makes the *raga* sound very different. A prominent example is that of *raga Marwa*.

2.83 *Nimisha* (H S winking, shutting the eye)

The minimal unit of measuring musical time equivalent to 9/32 of a second. It must however be remembered that in spite of similar exact descriptions and matching terminology, Indian performing tradition does not recognize the principle of absolute time.

2.84 *Nirgeet* (S)

The term, though not in general use, indicates an important musical practice of ancient lineage. The core meaning is 'song without words'. A performance of instrumental music without a song was described as *shuskageet*. A further sophistication of usage brought into circulation another term—*bahirgeet*, meaning a song irrelevant to the matter in a play. Such a song could be performed independently outside the performance of a play. A mythical explanation described *bahirgeet* as a composition couched in *laya, tala* etc. with *shushkashras*. As demons created *bahirgeet*, in competition with gods, the latter named the variety *bahirgeet*!

2.85 *Nishkala* (S)
A string instrument without drone or sympathetic strings (e.g. violin).
The opposite term is *sakala*.

2.86 *Nishabda* (S)
Indicates a soundless measurement of musical time in *tala*. *Sashabda*
is the opposite.

2.87 *Nyasa* (H S *nitaram* = in an effective manner + *asa* = to sit, to
stabilise)
A note in scale which clearly brings out the nature of a particular
raga. Mostly *nyasa* indicates a long duration of the note concerned.
With other terms such as *graha*, *apanyasa*, and *vinyasa*; *nyasa* was important in Indian music when *raga* was not a predominant concept.
When *raga* became the reigning concept, *nyasa* etc. made way for
vadi, *samvadi* and the related terms.

2.88 *Pada* (S)
In a rough translation *pada* means phrase.
1   In *raga*-music *pada* may be described as the minimal unit of notes
     indicative of a *raga*. In majority of cases, two notes suffice.
2   It also means portion of a musical composition consisting of
     meaningful language units. Of its two types, the *nibaddha* music
     is regulated by rules pertaining to metres etc. while *anibaddha* is
     free from such constraints. The latter is also known as *chur-
     napad*a while the former is known as *padya*.

2.89 *Padhant* (H *padhna* = to read, to recite)
In *pakhawaj*-music (and by extension in *tabla*-music) *padhant* indicates reciting aloud of compositions prior to playing them. Prior *padhant* is especially useful in case of compositions that consist of syllables which match meaningful words. Performance of a composition
subsequent to its *padhant* is called *bajant*. 'Translation' of meaningful
words by matching sound-syllables could be illustrated thus:
● *ganapati* =*gadikat*
● *jagat* =*digat*
● *shankar* =*dingan*

2.90 *Pakad* (H *pakadna* = to grapple, to hold)
A group of a minimal number of musical notes characteristic of a *raga*

is described as *pakad*. To performers and auditors alike, *pakad* offers
a good grip on the *raga*.

2.91 *Pata* (S)

The process of concretizing *tala* through procedures that employ
sound (e.g. claps). The opposite mode of operation employing
silence towards the same end is known as *shamya*. *Pata* connotes
sound-syllables (*akshara*) used to describe sounds producible from
various musical instruments.

2.92 *Pat* (H)

The process of acclerating tempi in a predetermined manner. The
short and long durations of the *pat* contribute to the basic patterns in
instrumental music.

2.93 *Poorab* (H S *poorva* = eastern)

A term employed to describe characteristic style of singing, playing
or dancing, especially in singing of *thumri*s and *tabla*-playing.
Region-wise the term indicates eastern areas of Uttar Pradesh.

2.94 *Pukar* (H *pukarna* = to call)

An effective way of intonation in vocal music. It consists of a
repeated use of a high note.

2.95 *Punjab ang*

Descriptive term employed to denote a characteristic way of singing
and *tabla*-playing. Flashy presentation, intricacy of design and occasional inclusion of folk idiom are some of the easily perceivable features.

2.96 *Raga* (S)

The traditional definition is wide enough to accommodate even har-
monic music within its ambit! It runs, '*Raga* is a group of stationary,
ascending or descending notes moving in violation of sequence or en-
joying other liberties. The notes are delightful to the hearts of men.'

In Hindustani music, *raga* as understood today is a result of process-
ing the scale to create generative, basic and melodic frameworks. The
contemporary *raga* formation has twelve notes as its foundation with
seven *shuddha* (authorized) and five *vikrut* (changed).

Important characteristics of *raga* stated by Pandit Bhatkhande are briefly described below:

1   No *raga* can be made of less than five notes.

2   A *raga* cannot omit both *madhyama* and *panchama*, that is the fourth and the fifth note.

3   A *raga* should not include two states (i.e. sharp and flat) of the same note consecutively.

4   Notes occurring in *raga* Bilawal are to be treated as *shuddha* for reference.

5   All *raga*s are principally classifiable into three groups according to their inclusion of *shuddha re, dha* or *komal re, dha* or *ga, ni*.

6   All *raga*s are bound by rules, pertaining to the *vadi*, that is the principal note.

7   A *raga* has its *poorvanga* or *uttaranga* as the chief area of elaboration according to the location of the *vadi*.

8   Relationship of *raga* with diurnal as well as seasonal time-cycle is a defining characteristic.

9   To determine the *raga*-time relationship, the importance of *tivra madhyama* in a particular *raga* serves as a prime indicator.

10   In accordance with their association with either of the twilight periods, *raga*s are classified in two broad divisions. *Raga*s belonging to the two twilights display structural features describable as question-answer.

11   In *a raga*, *vivadi* is not an omitted note. It is used sparingly and judiciously to add colour to the *raga*.

12   Raga in the twilight periods follow a sequence vis-a-vis the time of their performance. The group of *raga*s including *komal re,dha* are followed by those consisting of *re, dha, ga* and *ni shuddha*. Finally come *raga*s using *ga, ni komal*. Ragas with *sa, ma, pa* as important notes precede the twilight *raga*s.

13   *Raga*s strong in *poorvanga* are strong in ascending movement; those strong in *uttaranga* are strong in descent.

14   To mix/combine *raga*s and *ragini*s is a legitimate procedure of enriching *raga* music.

It is possible to classify *raga*s in many ways. Classifications throw an important light on the formative elements of the *raga* corpus taken as a whole. Some classifications along with the criteria they employ are mentioned below:

a   *Sampoorna* = seven notes
     Shadava = six notes
     Odava = five notes

The criterion is the number of notes a *raga* includes.

b   *shuddha* = pure, original
     chhayalaga = with a shadow of other ragas
     sankeerna = being a mixture of many ragas
     The criterion is the type of grammatical exclusiveness a *raga* enjoys.

c   *pratargeya* = sung/rendered at mornings
     sayamgeya = sung/rendered in evenings
     The criterion is the time of the day at which a *raga* is to be performed.

d   *re-dha (shuddha)* included
     re-dha (komal) included
     ga-ni (komal) included
     The criterion applied is the existence of a particular structural weightage.

e   *prachalita* = in easy circulation
     aprachalita = rare circulation
     The criterion is the vogue enjoyed.

f   *sarala* = simple
     vakra = convoluted
     The criterion is the movemental contour displayed prominently by a *raga*.

g   *alapapradhan* = conducive to elaborations in show tempo
     tanapradhan = conducive to elaborations in fast tempi
     The criterion applied is the prominence given to different elaborational phases and the associated tempi.

h   *poorvangapradhan* = strong in the first half
     uttarangapradhan = strong in the second half
     The criterion is the prominence enjoyed by one or the other half of an octave.

i   *aam raga* = expansive raga
     dhun raga = raga with limited inbuilt melodic structuring
     The criterion employed is the elaborational potentialities of different *raga*s.

j   spring = *Hindol raga*
     summer = *Deepak raga*
     monsoon = *Megha raga*
     winter = *Bhairava raga*
     hemant = *Shri raga*
     shishir = *Malkauns raga*

The criterion employed is the seasonal associations a *raga* enjoys in the tradition.

k   Many *raga*s are classified according to their place of origin.

l   *Raga*s are also classified according to an implied sexual symbolism.

m   Some *raga*s proclaim their ethnic origin.

2.97 *Raganga paddhati*

Pandit Narayan Moreshwar Khare, a disciple of Pandit Vishnu Digambar Paluskar, attempted a new system of *raga* classification called *raganga*. He maintained that as a first step towards a scientific classification, *raga*s that fulfill all the fundamental conditions of *raga*-formation are to be identified. Other *raga*s are created by exploiting selected aspects (*anga*) of the fundamental *raga*s. He advocated twenty-six groups formulated according to his theory.

2.98 *Raga-ragini*

The paired term operates at various levels.

At the metaphysical level it mirrors the *Shiva-Shakti* or *Purush-Prakriti* pair to represent the male-female principle in music.

The musicological tradition refers to six major *raga*s and thirty-six *ragini*s. It is possible that the aesthetic theories of *Natyashastra* advocating the *nayaka-nayika* differentiation influenced the musical thinking to result into *raga-ragini*s.

Various criteria have been advocated to differentiate *raga*s from *ragini*s. A few are noted here:

a   The original seasonal *raga*s, six in number, are the *raga*s, others being *ragini*s.

b   *Raga*s are rendered in slow movement and are serious in mood. *Ragini*s are light-hearted and fast in pace.

c   Name of the *raga-ragini*s indicate their genders.

d   *Raga*s have larger tonal intervals as opposted to the *ragini*s which have them smaller.

It appears that *raga-ragini* classification was one of the ways in which the growing *raga*-corpus was sought to be systematized. After the *mela* or the that principle gained ascendency, *raga-ragini* classification become redundant.

2.99 *Ritusangeet* (H S *ritu* = season + *sangeet* = music)

Indian musicology firmly associatee six *raga*s with six seasons of a single calendar year. According to the *Hanuman-mata* the correspondence is:

Season	Raga	Months
Grishma	*Deepak*	*Jyeshtha-Ashadh*
Varsha	*Megh*	*Shravan-Bhadrapad*
Sharad	*Bhairav*	*Ashwin-Kartik*
Hemant	*Malkauns*	*Margashish-Pousha*
Shishir	*Shri*	*Magh-Phalgun*
Vasant	*Hindol*	*Chaitra-Vaishakh*

2.100 *Sachala* (S shiftable)
1   *Sachalaswara:*notes with variations such as *komal, tivra* etc. *Shadja* (*sa*) and *Panchama* (*pa*) are regarded unchangeable.
2   *Sachala that:* an arrangement of shiftable frets effected to facilitate an easy use of variations of notes. See *achala that..*

2.101 *Sakala vadya*
Instrument which provides drone as well as melody.

2.102 *Sampoorna* (S complete)
Usually refers to an arrangement of notes which includes all the seven notes of the gamut.

2.103 *Samvadatatva* (H S *samvada* = harmony + *tatva* = element)
An important musicological principle of organizing melodic material by establishing mandatory relationships between two or more elements. The principle may become applicable to rhythmic material though some reinterpretation of the concept and employement of new terminology might be necessary.

Primarily and traditionally the first application of the *samvadatatva* is to employ two notes distanced by nine or thirteen microtonal intervals (*shrutis*). Such pairs display a special degree of consonance. An application of the first-fifth relationship (called *shadja-panchama bhava*) or the first-fourth (called *shadja-madhyama bhava*) makes available the consonant pairs.

Secondarily *samvadatatva* may refer to similarities in structures. For example, the two triads, *sa, re, ga,* and *pa, dha, ni,* reveal a constructional correspondence.

Thirdly the *samvadatatva* is also applied to *raga*s because they are often formulated to function as questions and answers. For example,

Deshkar, a morning *raga* and *Bhoopa*, a *raga* for early night, exemplify the *samvadatatva* because in spite of similar ascent-descent, the two move differently on account of shifts in emphases.

2.104 *Sangeet* (H S *sam* = good + *geet* = sung)
Generic term for a combined manifestation of the sung, the played and the danced.

It is significant to note that the western term music also indicates a combined operation of performing arts later treated as separate entities.

2.105 *Sangeetlekhana*, (H S *sangeet* = music + *lekhana* = writing)
The proper term to indicate notation of music in India. *Swaralekhana*, the term often used, seems to be a literal translation of the western term notation. The latter would rule out inclusion of the linguistic texts, sound-syllables employed by melodic and rhythmic instruments etc.

2.106 *Sangeetshastra* (H S *sangeet* = music + *shastra* = science)
Musicology, earlier known as *gandharva-tatva*. It includes studies broadly classifiable in three categories as shown:

1   Directly related to study and performance of music:
   a. Characteristics of *raga*, *tala*, forms of music and musical instruments
   b. Rules related to elaboration of musical ideas, rhythmic as well as melodic
   c. Playing techniques for the four types of instruments
   d. Musical embellishments and *gamaka*s
   e. Musical scales and their manipulations

2   Indirectly connected with performance:
   a. Metrics
   b. Notation
   c. Musical mnenonics
   d. Musical aesthetics

3   Having no connection with performance:
   a. Music and mathematics
   b. Musical history

2.107 *Sansthana* (S)
Synonymous with *that* (>) and *makam* and *mela* (>). The term was
first used by Lochana in his work *Ragatarangini* (1160).

2.108 *Saptaka* (S a group of seven)
The group of basic seven notes from *shadja* to *nishad*. As the count
proceeds in an ascending order the eighth note is counted and becomes
the first note of the next *saptaka*, hence it is not included in counting
the first *saptaka*. More plausible reason is that the count is related to
the intervals between two notes, and not to the notes themselves.

Three generally accepted *saptaka*s are the *mandra* (bass), *madhya*
(medium) and *tara* (treble) respectively. The names of notes within a
saptaka are:

Note-name	Shortform	Position	Meaning
shadja	*sa*	first	that from which six are born
rishabha	*re*	second	-
gandhara	*ga*	third	-
madhyama	*ma*	fourth	middle
panchama	*pa*	fifth	fifth
dhaivata	*dha*	sixth	-
nishada	*ni*	seventh	-

The order of notes as indicated above was accepted sometime
during the medieval period. The early gamut, arranged in a descending order had less number of notes.

2.109 *Shabdalapa* (H S *shabd*a = articualated sound + *alap*)
The *alapa*s(-) superimposed on the words from the song. *Bol-alapa* is
synonymous with *shabdalapa*.

2.110 *Shabdadosha* (*shabda* = articulated sound + *dosha* = demerit)
Indian musicology pays adequate attention to merits and demerits of
singers. Unfortunately all descriptions are not clear today and overlaps
between terms and concepts are confusing. The eight *dosha*s are:
i   *ruksha* = dry
ii   *sphurita* = with breaks
iii *nissara* = lacking in inner strength
iv   *kakolika* = like a crow

v *keti* = ranging over three octaves but without quality
vi *keni* = experiencing difficulties in *tara and mandra* elaborations
vii *krishna* = weak
viii *bhagna* = lacking in effect
   Shabdaguna is the antonym.

2.111 *Shabdaguna* (*shabda* = articulated sound + *guna* = merit)
See *shabdadosha* (>)
   The fifteen *shabdagunas* are:
1 *mrishta* = filling ears without causing pain
2 *madhura* = full in all the three octaves
3 *chehala* = possessing six characteristics
   The six are:
   shasta = easily perceivable
   proudha = mature
   natisthool = not thick
   natikrish = not thin
   snigdha = loving
   ghana = solid
4 *tristhana* = clear and pleasant in three octaves
5 *sukhavaha* = delightful to the mind
6 *prachura* = thick
7 *gadha* = strong, powerful
8 *sharowak* = possessing carrying power
9 *karuna* = capable of producing pathos
10 *ghana* = possessing inner strength
11 *snigdha* = loving
12 *shlakshna* = continuous
13 *raktibhav* = entertaining
14 *chhaviman* = clearly articulated
15 *komala* = soft

2.112 *Shadjachalana* (S *shadja* = produced from six organs + *chalana* = to shift)
To shift the beginning note without altering the sequence of notes.

2.113 *Sparsha* (S touch)
An important playing technique in string-music. The forefinger of the left hand is kept on a fret and the next fret is touched by the middle finger.

2.114 *Sthana* (S place)

According to the tradition, chest (*hridaya*), throat (*kantha*), and head (*shira*) are responsible for producing bass (*mandra*), medium (*madhya*) and treble (*tara*) octaves respectively in vocal music. *Hridaya* etc. are called *sthana*s. With a slight shift the term is also applied generally to mean an octave and hence the usage is extended to instrumental ranges.

2.115 *Sruti* (S one which is heard)

Microtonal intervals for which Hindsutani art music is well known.

The minimal notional unit employed to measure the progressively increasing pitches of notes within a musical scale is called *sruti*. It is so called because *sruti* is determined chiefly through a fine auditory sensibility. Sounds falling within a scale are infinite. The reason why the number of *sruti*s is limited to twenty-two is yet to be conclusively stated. According to tradition, the twenty-two *sruti*s are further grouped into five classes.

Almost every aspect of the sruti phenomenon has raised controversies that are raging even today. Important controvertial positions are:

a   The *sruti*s are not equal

b   Every note is established on its first *sruti*

c   It is possible to state the *sruti* system in terms of the western acoustic concepts of frequency, cents etc.

d   The conventional natural scale in the western system and the Hindustani *bilawal that* would appear to correspond if the modern acoustical explanation of the western scale and the *sruti* tradition are shown to be similar.

Diametrically opposite views have been expressed on each of these and similar points argued.

2.116 *Sur* (H S *swara* = note)

1   *Shadja* the first note of the Indian *saptaka* (>). May be understood as a 'key' in the western sense of the term.

2   Drone.

2.117 *Sushira* (adj. S perforated, full of holes)

Aerophones i.e. wind instruments, an ancient category of musical instruments. Some important technical/structural terms are:

phoonk = blown wind

nada-chhidra = sound hole

chabhi = key
mukh patti = reed
mukha = mouth
tumba = gourd
penda = base
pet = belly
kalash = top-portion (ref. conch)
nali = pipe
nabhi = navel, centre (ref. conch)

2.118 *Swara* (H S sound, noise)
Musical note. All sounds are not musical and all musical sounds are not notes. Musical sounds are called *srutis* and *srutis* which are members of scales are known as *swaras*. The first and the fifth notes, called *shadja 'sa'* and *panchama 'pa'* are regarded immutable in Indian musicology. The remaining five notes have two states each, thus resulting in the present twelve notes. In this manner at the first level, the *swaras* are stable and unalterable or unchanged.

The changes in *swaras* are brought about in two ways:
1   By application of the *murchhana* (>) process.
2   By changing the established microtonal values.

For example, to shift the beginning of the *saptaka* to *re* instead of from the *sa* would give us *komal* states of *ga* and *ni*. This is the *murchhana-* way.

An example of the second method is to highten the pitch-values of the earlier notes by borrowing microtonal degrees of the higher note. It is obvious that changes introduced in this matter are notional but the changes in intervals and demarcation points help in permutation and combination of *swaras*.

Many classifications of *swaras* prevail, though all of them do not continue to have the same contemporary relevance. For example:

1   *Udatta, swarita* and *anudatta* (vedic music), *graha, nyasa, ansha* (*nibaddha* music), *komal, tivra* (lowered and heightened), *chetana, achetana, mishra,* (respectively referred to human voice, lifeless objects and a combination of both as producers of *swaras*.)
2   *swara dhun*: a group of notes composed/executed/elaborated without having to conform to the restraints of *raga*-grammar. It may or may not have a *tala*.

	PALUSKAR-SYSTEM	BHATKHANDE-SYSTEM
1. To indicate Lower Octave (Shuddha Swaras)	•ni •dha •pa •ma	•ni •dha •pa •ma
2. To indicate Medium Octave (Shuddha Swaras)	sa re ga ma (No symbol is used)	sa re ga ma (No symbol is used)
3. To indicate Upper Octave (Shuddha Swaras)	re ga ma pa	•re •ga •ma •pa
4. To indicate 'Komal' i.e. Flat Swaras	re ga dha ni	re ga dha ni
5. To indicate 'Tivra' i.e. Sharp Swaras	ma	ma
6. Division of Time : (a) To indicate 'Sam' i.e. the first 'Matra' (beat)	'ؘ' symbol is used. below the note-name	'X' symbol is used below the note-name
(b) To indicate kal or khali	'+' symbol is used below the note-name Respective number is put under the note-name	'o' symbol is used below the note-name Respective number is put under the note-name
(c) To indicate Tali (Clap): 2nd. 3rd. 4th & so on.....	'x' symbol is used below the note-name. (The symbol is named as 'Chatasra')	
7. To indicate four Matras,	'ᔓ' symbol is used below the note-name. (The symbol is named as 'Guru')	
8. To indicate two Matras,		

9. To indicate one Matra, '—' symbol is used below the note-name (The symbol is named as 'Laghu'.)

10. *Division of Matras* :

(a) To indicate ½ Matra, '0' symbol is used below the note-name (The symbol is named as 'Drut'.)

(b) To indicate ¼th Matra, '◡' symbol is used below the note-name (The symbol is named as 'Anu-Drut'.)

(c) To indicate ⅛th Matra, '◡◡' symbol is used below the note-name

(d) To indicate ⅓rd and ⅙th Matra. ⅓ and ⅙ numbers are put below note-name respectively

11. To indicate a sustained use of word— ja ●●vo ●●

12. To indicate meend. i.e. sustained use of a Swara ma s pa s s dha ja s s s vo s s

ma— pa— —dha

13. To indicate Kan-Swaras i.e. Grace Notes—

ga ma
sa re ga

ma pa dha ni

ga ma
sa re ga

14. To indicate continuous tonal production—

ma pa dha ni

15. Notes brought together with a curve below are to be sung or played in one Matra e.g.
dha ni sa sa ni dha pa

(pa) = dha pa ma pa
or
(re) = ga re sa re

16. Bracketed note, is to be used along with the succeeding and preceding notes respectively. in one Matra

(pa) = dha pa ma pa
or
(re) = ga re sa re

2.119 *Swaralipi* (H S *swara* = note + *lipi* = script)
The nineteenth century named notation as *swaralipi*.

A skeletal system of notation was in operation in ancient India but *swaralipi* came into prominence and use in the latter part of the nineteenth century. Many systems were devised and advocated but the two which gained following were formulated by Pandit Vishnu Digamber Paluskar (1900) and Pandit Vishnu Narayan Bhatkhande (1910). The major notational signs employed by them are:

2.120 *Swaradnyana* (H S *swara* = note + *dnyana* = knowledge)
Sensitivity or otherwise to tunefulness. Though the modern concept of just noticeable difference may apply, *swaradnyana* has nothing to do with the sense of absolute pitch. A finer sense of the subtleties of tonal intervals is described by adding the adjective *sookshma* (subtle) to *swaradnyana*.

2.121 *Swarasanchalana* (H S *swara* = note + *sanchalana* = to move)
Changing the keynote to build a new melody etc.

2.122 *Swayambhu* (H S *swayam* = oneself + *bhu* = to become)
A term coined to refer to the harmonics created by and heard from the first and the fourth string of a *tanpura* (>). Also applied to similar other sounds.

2.123 *Syunt* (S)
One of the three basic techniques of tone-production, the two other being *gamaka* and *meend*. It involves passing smoothly to a higher note from a lower. Continuity of an upward movement characterizes the *syunt*, a downward movement indicates the *meend* (>).

2.124 *Takrari bol* (*takrar* = repetition + *bol* = meaningful words)
Very often a part of a song needs repetition for effect. To facilitate the repetition and to help in meeting the demands of the *tala*-cycle, short words not originally included in the song (e.g. *ab* = now, *are* = oh you, *re* = yes, my love) are added by the singer on the spur of the moment. These are known as *takrari bol*.

2.125 *Tala* (H S *tal* = the palm of the hand)
Amarkosh succinctly defines *tala* as a measure employed in the act of keeping time.

Ancient Vedic recitation required use of different pitch-levels leading to formation of the scale range. The recitation inevitably needed control and manipulation of the recited words to ensure faultless prosodic arrangements. Scale-manipulation and time-frame exploitation together led to metre as well as to *tala*. On this background it is understandable that a number of *tala*-terms bear a mark of a genetic relationship with linguistic and literary terminology.

Tala is that measure of time which through the process of lengthening and shortening of durations, controls the manifestation of singing, instrumental music and dance. It becomes recognizable through the employment of sound, silence, rest, variation of intensity and tempi.

Infinite number of *tala*s are theoretically possible though musicological texts have settled on 108, probably to correspond with the mythical one hundred and eight dances of Lord Shiva, the patron deity of all performing arts.

The major characteristics of *tala* are codified and they are collectively known as *dashaprana*s. They are briefly explained below:

1   *Kala* (time): Temporality as opposed to spatiality is the essence.
2   *Anga*: Reportedly refers to six sections of *tala* described according to their respective durational values. The significance of the term is not clear.
3   *Kriya* (action): Connotes procedures adopted to keep time by using sounds, silences, hand movements etc.
4   *Marga* (path): Refers to the relative density of notes in a duration of one *matra*. Six ways of manipulating the duration are indicated. However the *marga*-concept as such is no more in circulation in performing traditions.
5   *Jati* (kind): A *tala*-unit may consist of three, four, five divisions or combinations of these. They are known as *tisra, chatusra, khanda* and *mishra* respectively.
6   *Kala:* Subdivisions or segments, which constitute the essence of any significant patterning activity.
7   *Graha* (to grapple, to grip): Taking to or joining with. The *graha* of *tala* in use is described as *sama, atita, anagata* or *vishama* depending on the relationship the onset of melody has with the beginning of *tala*. *Sama-graha* is the correspondence of the two, *atita-graha* is over-reaching of the *tala*-onset by the melody onset, *anagata-graha* is the underreaching. *Vishama-graha* is an indifferent relationship between the two.
8   *Laya* (tempo): It is the equidistance between the beats of a *tala*.

9   *Yati* (a pause in a metre): Ways in which tempi are distributed in
     a *tala*. *Sama-yati* is to have the same *laya* in the beginning, mid-
     dle and end of a *tala*. *Srota/srotogata yati* is successive doubling
     of the tempi in the beginning, the middle and the end-sections of
     a *tala*.
     Pipilika: Characterized by random slow, medium and fast move-
     ments.
     Gopuccha (cow's tail): Fast, slow and fast in successive sections.
10   *Prastar* (elaboration): At this stage of the evolution of a *tala*,
     forms of rhythm-music take over.
     It must be admitted however, that the minute systematization has
not been assiduously followed in the contemporary performing tradition. A new set of terms rather tenuously connected with the
dashaprana systematization has come into circulation. Some important
concepts in the present-day *tala*-system are explained below:

- *Sam*: The first and usually the stressed beat of the *tala*-cycle.
- *Kala:* The unstressed or the weakly stressed division-point. It is
  usually indicated by an outward and a downward movement of
  an open palm when *tala* is being marked by hand-movements. It
  is also known as *khali* (empty).
- *Matra:* Measure of the duration between two normal divisions of
  a *tala*.
- *Khand:* Sections in which *tala*s are divided.
- *Bhari* : *Tala*, when taken as a whole exhibits sections relatively
  more and less sonorous (due to the character of the sound-syllables included). The more sonorous sections are described as
  bhari.
- *Khali* : Sections of a *tala* described as less sonorous. Sometimes
  the term is also used rather confusingly in the sense of *kala* (see
  above).
- *Tali:* The clap-point in the *tala*-pattern when the latter is marked
  by hand-movements. To indicate the point with a clap is to suggest that the beat so marked represents the sonorous element.
  These points are to be matched by appropriately sonorous
  sound-syllables when the *tala* is played on an instrument.
- *Theka:* In order to create varied sound-patterns, a *tala*-design
  needs to be expressed through different sound-syllables. Thus
  one *tala* may have many *thekas*, depending of course on the
  potentialities of the instrument employed.
- *Bol:* Syllables formed by instrumental sound. Richness of any instrumental language depends on the availability of identifiable,
  reproducible, isolable and minimal sound-patterns which, if so

employed, become sound-syllables.

2.126 *Talim* (A teaching, towrds expertise)
Learning and teaching of music according to the norms of the *guru-shishya* tradition.

2.127 *Tana* (S *tan* = to stretch, expand)
The etymology suggests that melody or *raga* is expanded through the use of *tana*s. The term possibly owes its origin to a technique in instrumental music whereby notes are added to a melody by stretching a string.

Two main varieties of *tana*s are mentioned, *shuddha* (pure), in which notes are employed in sequence and *kuta* (puzzling) wherein notes are employed out of sequence. These two basic structural strategies, when applied to the scale-range, yield seven types identified in the ancient tradition as follows:

archika = consisting of one note
gathiku − consisting of two notes
samika = consisting of three notes
swarantara = consisting of four notes
odava = consisting of five notes
shadava = consisting of six notes
sampoorna = consisting of seven notes

Thus understood it appears that *murchhana* (>) is also to be considered a *tana*. However it has been argued that while *tana* enjoys only the ascending order, *murchhana* enjoys both the ascending and descending orders. Applying the formula rigorously to scales evolved from each of the seven notes, musicology has enumerated the number of possible *tana*s to a total of 5040! It is however obvious that combined with words, *gamaka*s, tempi-changing etc. an infinite number of *tana*s are possible. The contemporary tradition displays a rather confused classification but the rich variety of *tana*s employed in performance is well reflected in the terminology used. Some of the terms are noted:

1   *Utarti* (descending) = *sa ni sa, dha pa dha, ma ga ma, . . .*
2   *Kaki* = in a crow-like voice
3   *Khuli* = using open vowel-sounds, especially 'a'
4   *Jabadi* = produced with the help of jaw movements
5   *Tangan* (hanging) = produced with the use of the vowel-sound 'ee'
6   *Palti* (inversion) = *sa re ga ma, ma ga re sa*

2.128 *Taranga-vadya* (S *taranga* = ripple + *vadya* = instrument)
A new addition to the instrumental typology.

Ghana (>) instruments such as *jalataranga* are able to produce musical notes otherwise not producible in the categories. A special plea has been made to create a category comprising them.

2.129 *Tarata* (H S *tara* = high)
An acoustic term refering to the parameter of pitch, the two other parameters being intensity and timbre.

2.130 *Tata* (H S *tata* = stringed)
Refers to the category of musical instruments described as chordophones. Some structural/technical terms are:

　　dhancha = skeleton
　　gaj = bow
　　kaman/dhanush = curved bow
　　ghodi/ghudach = bridge
　　mijrab = wire plectrum
　　nakhi = wire plectrum
　　tantri/tar = string
　　tumb/tumbi/kaddu/tumba = gourd round/flattened
　　dan/dandi = stem
　　khunti = peg
　　tabli = disc to cover the resonator
　　sarika/parda = fret
　　kon/trikon/jawa = wooden/metal striker of strings
　　tarab/taraf = sympathetic strings
　　mooth = grip
　　adhar/apar shikha = lower/upper end
　　chikari = high pitched accessory strings
　　pet = belly
　　kamar = waist
　　baj ka tar = main string (also called nayaki tar)
　　ghat = clay pot
　　patra/patrika = plate
　　meru = edge
　　kakubha = crooked end-piece of a string-instrument
　　shalaka = small and thin stick
　　keel = a wooden or metal nail
　　jawari = cotton string inserted between string and the bridge

kamrika = a curved bow (small)
shanku = cone, conical instrumental part
nabhi = navel, centre
chibuk = chin/chin-rest
khal = leather covering
langot = a triangular thin plate
atak = end-part beyond which a string does not extend
gulu = gum used to stick wooden strips etc.
sajawat = decoration
gardan = neck
jod ki tar = accompanying string customarily tuned in the key selected by the instrumentalist

2.131 *Tatavanaddha (tata* = stringed + *avanaddha* = covered)
Stringed instruments with a membrane, it is argued, need to be described as *tatvaanaddha*. This appears a better substitute for the ancient *vitata*.

2.132 *Teep* (H *teepna* = to utter forcefully)
Today *teep* means higher octave. The term is probably connected with the medieval description of the important instrument *bansuri* (>). According to the medieval tradition the sound-hole used to produce high notes (located near the blow hole) was known as *teepa*.

2.133 *Tenaka*
According to the medieval tradition meaningless sound-syllables such as *tena, na, ri* were employed as components of musical genres. They were regarded auspicious. Even today musical genres such as *tarana, chaturang, ras* employ meaningless sound-syllables though they seem to have lost the auspicious aura.

2.134 *Thap* (H *thapna* S *sthapana* = installation)
A characteristic playing technique is described as *thap* in *avanaddha* (>) *instruments such as tabla, pakhawaj* etc. The technique involves lifting up the palm immediately after it has struck the drum-face. This is designed to produce an open sound. The stroke requires a skilful co-ordination of finger-closure, placement of fingers on *syahi* (>) and the angle at which the membrane is struck. Hence *thap* is regarded as a test of the technical virtuosity attained by the performer.
Pakhawaj relies more on *thap* hence the style of playing it is aptly

described as *thapiya baj.*

2.135 *That* (H *thath* = group)

A sequential and complete scale of the seven primary notes in ascending and descending orders. If one combines and permutates the *vikrut* (changed, that is, *komal, tivra* etc.) within the septet, a number of *that*s are possible. Vyankatmakhi derived seventy two *that*s and explained the derivation in his *Chaturdandiprakashika* (1660 A.D.) Drawing on many earlier formulations Pandit Bhatkhande propounded a system of ten main *that*s and one hundred and ninety five *raga*s derived from them. It is clear that *that*s resulted from a systematization of *raga*s which existed prior to the *that*-formulation. However Pandit Bhatkhande proceeded to name each that after a prominent *raga* in the same that. In this way the prominent *raga* came to be installed as a *janak* (creator) *raga* and other *raga*s in the same that became *janya* (created) *raga*s. The *janak raga* is also described as *ashraya* (support) or *melkarta* (creator of the *mela) raga.*

Historically speaking that was in all probability a necessity for accompanists on string instruments who had to establish all notes (including the *vikruta)* in one octave-range to facilitate changes in the fundamental. This is why they resorted to the immovable *(achala) that.*

Prior to Bhatkhande, Bhavbhatta's *Anup-sangitratnakara* mentioned *that*s and *raga*s subsumed under them.

Sansthana, mela and *thath* are synonyms.

2.136 *Tivrata* (H S *tivra* = intense + *ta)*

An acoustic term for the intensity of sound as contrasted with the two other parameters, namely its pitch and timbre.

2.137 *Tuk* (H tuk = piece)

A number of terms such as *amsha, kali, dhatu, charan* and *tuk* are employed to indicate parts of larger musical entities. Compositional genres such as *dhrupad, khayal* etc. have a definite number of *tuk*s as a distinguishing trait. The term is also used in instrumental music.

2.138 *Upaj* (v. H *upajna* = to be created)

To improvise on a short phrase from a musical composition – the product being described as *upaj.*

2.139 *Ucchara* (S utterance, pronunciation, declaration, or v. H *uccharna* = to utter)
Beginning of a *tala* in vocal or instrumental music.

2.140 *Uthan/n* (H S *utthana* = the act of rising or standing up, getting up)
A short preparatory piece in *tabla/pakhawaj* music to be played prior to playing a *tala* or *theka*.

2.141 *Vadana* (H S *vad* = to sound, to converse)
All instrumental music is described as *vadana*. Five kinds of *vadana*s are defined:

 tatva = following the song strictly.
 anugata = following the song but also consisting of independent playing.
 ogha = repeating the entire musical content of the earlier eleboration at the end of a composition independently.
 chitravritti = overshadowing the song.
 dakshinavritti = overshadowed by the song.

 A *vadana* without a song is described as *nirgeet* or *shushkavadya*.

2.142 *Vadi* (H S *vad* = to converse, to sound)
Inter-relationship of notes within the *saptak* needs to be regulated if musical activity is to lead to significant patterns.
 Notes of a *saptaka* are therefore classified into four groups known as *vadi*, *samvadi*, *anuvadi* and *vivadi* respectively.
 In its stabilized and unelaborated state *saptaka* does not have the four classes in operation because in a *saptaka* all notes are of equal importance at all times. The foursome comes into existence when the *saptaka* becomes dynamic and when it is developed for patterning. It is to be remembered that the quartet came into reckoning only after the *murchhana* (>) system of creating new bases for musical development was replaced by a system which established all notes in one octave-range. Briefly the four classes can be explained as follows:
 vadi = The most important note.
 samvadi = Note next in importance to the *vadi*. It is located in that half of the octave which does not include the *vadi*.
 anuvadi = All notes other than *vadi* and *samvadi*.

vivadi = Notes entirely omitted or sparingly used (in a *raga*).

2.143 *Vaditra* (S)
An older term for musical instruments--*atodya* was yet another ancient and synonymous term.

2.144 *Vadya* (S)
An instrument to express musical sound and movement. The definition appears to be wide enough to include human voice. Indian musicology however holds that human voice is not man-made and hence it constitutes a class by itself. Thus the term *vadya* connotes four man-made and one divinely created *vadya*. Tradition divides *vadya*s into four classes, namely, *tata, avanaddha, sushira* and *ghana*. *Vitata* was once regarded as a separate category. *Tatavanaddha* and *tarangvadya* categories are advocated by modern thinkers.

2.145 *Vaggeyakara* (S *vak* = noice + *geya* singable)
Composer. The word aspect of a composition is known as *vak* or *matu* and the musical aspect as *geya* or *dhatu*. A person proficient in both is known as *vaggeyakara*.

2.146 *Varjya/varjita* (S)
Note/s omitted from a particular *raga* in conformity with the relevant rules.

2.147 *Varna* (S)
1   A letter expressed trough combinations of vowel and consonant sounds.
2   *Jati* i.e. the basic way of bringing together or combining musical notes. Four basic strategies of organizing tonal material in a melodic treatment are laid down:
     a. *sthayi* = repetition or prolongation of a single note. e.g. *sa, sa, sa.*
     b. *aroha* = arrangement of notes in an ascending order on the dimension of pitch. It is also known as *anuloma*. e.g. *sa, re, ga.*
     c. *avaroha* = arrangement of notes in a descending order on the dimension of pitch e.g. *sa, ni, dha* etc. It is also known as *viloma*.
     d. *sanchari* = employment of notes by incorporating all the three possibilities described. *Sanchari* may allow notes in *krama* (that

is, in the grammatically sanctioned order) or as *santar* (that is omitting or stepping over certain notes).

The *varna*s are developed further by using embellishments etc.

As fundamental strategies, *varna*s are relevant to recitation as well as singing. Hence, *pathya* (recitation) too has four types of *varna*s. They are:

    udatta = high pitched
    anudatta = low pitched
    swarita = having sustained high or low pitches
    kampita = vibratory
    All *varna*s are employable in any octave.

2.148 *Vidara* (S inundation, overflowing)

Notes within a *raga* have a certain flow. To open new possibilities of elaboration by changing their sequence etc. and yet to keep the flow uninterrupted is known as *vidara*.

2.149 *Viloma* (S reverse, contrary)

The inversed melodic sequence of notes, that is, *avaroha*.

2.150 *Vistara* (S)

Elaboration or development of melodic or rhythmic ideas in music. *Prastara,* a term that appears to be synonymous with *vistara* needs to be confined to highly regulated elaborations especially in rhythm-music.

2.151 *Vritti* (mode of action)

A term used to classify three basic interrelationships between song and instrumental music in a combined rendering:

i	*chitra vritti:*	instrument leads, song follows
ii	*vartik vritti:*	song and instruments are equal in importance
iii	*dakshina vritti:*	the song leads and instruments follow

3 Musical Instruments

This section has a limited purpose of describing instruments active on the Hindustani concert stage. Not more than a score are in operation and all of them do not share musical prosperity equally.

Hindustani musical instruments carry out three tasks. They present music solo, provide tonal or rhythmic accompaniment or produce drone. Some instruments are capable of accomplishing more than one task while some have an exclusive application. But the occasions when an instrument performs two or more roles at the same time are rare. In other words considerable specialization is displayed in Hindustani instrumental usage.

While in solo or accompanying mode, instruments have to explore one of the two dimensions chiefly: melodic or rhythmic. However when instruments make music, the voice does not take up the mantle of accompaniment, thus stressing the primacy of vocal music. This, in fact, is one of the distinguishing marks of art music.

The general abundance of musical instruments has inevitably led to classification which in turn has led to a number of ways of classifying the instruments. Contemporary musical practice is fairly well-explained by the traditional four-fold classification. Instruments are accordingly classified by identifying the major sound-producing agent. Therefore, *tata* (with string), *ghan* (solid), *sushir* (with holes), and *avanaddha* (membrane-covered) form the four major classes. One more class is also mentioned sometimes, namely, *vitata* i.e. with strings and membrane-covered (bodies). Many other classifications advocated today are relevant at more academic levels.

One medieval classification is of interest for its performance-orientation. It held that instruments are classifiable according to the lead they followed. For example, instruments that followed dance were described as *nrittyanuga*, those guided by vocal music were called *geetanuga*, and those played independently, were set apart as *prithag-*

vadya. Even today it would be difficult to brush aside the functional bias displayed in this classification as irrelevant!

In theory it is possible to hold that any instrument can find a place in any set-up, Yet, in reality, instrumental mobility is considerably restricted. Firstly, the acoustic properties of every instrument limit its circulation. Secondly, the melodic nature of Hindustani music places a premium on instruments capable of a sustained tonal production. Thirdly, non-musical cultural associations also play a part in determining the scope allowed to an instrument. Taboos and sanctions have a role in music which, after all, forms one segment of the total life-pattern.

To know about an instrument is useful. It helps to have right expectations from it and its user. Information about instruments is conducive to reception of music made by them. Instruments are objects and they also store social information. However such information is often tenuously linked to the actual performance. It is, therefore, proposed to select the following aspects for description/discussion in the present section:

1 Name/s
2 Etymology
3 Classification
4 Legend
5 Constructional features
6 History
7 Hold, posture and playing technique
8 Tuning method

3.1 *Bansuri*
- *Bansuri,* flute
- (H *bans* S *vamsha* = bamboo)
- *Sushira*

Loosely referred to as *murali, venu, algooz, vamshi,* flute etc. However these different names should be specifically *applied* to definite kinds. As far as concert music is concerned, *bansuri* is an influential instrument. Its two main varieties namely, horizontal and vertical, clearly indicate origin from a bamboo. In fact other names such as *venu, vamshi* also reflect the fact. The horizontal *bansuri* is aptly called *ad-bansuri, ad* meaning that which is held in front of the eyes, from left to right or vice-versa.

Kalidasa (634 A.D.) in his *Kumarasambhava* has recorded a legend

Bansuri

about the instrument. A black bee bore through a slender bamboo. Wind blowing through it created so haunting a musical sound that the music-loving demi-gods, *kinnaras,* cut away the portion to make an instrument.

Horizontal *bansuri* is a simple cylindrical bamboo tube of a uniform bore. Closed at one end it *ranges* in length from 30 cms to 75 cms. Longer *bansuri*s are lower in pitch and deeper in tone. A few centimeters from the closed end is located the blow-hole or embouchure through which the player blows. There are six to eight holes placed in a straight line along the body enabling the player to vary the sounding length to produce notes of different pitches. The *bansuri* has a compass of about two and a half octaves. Unlike similar Western instruments the Hindustani *bansuri* has no mechanical valves or keys. Though flutes can be made of various types of wood, as well as of ivory and metals, Hindustani art musicians prefer *bansuri*s made of bamboo available in Assam.

The prototype of the instrument boasts of a long history. During the Vedic period it was employed in *samgana,* the earliest musico-religious recitations in India. The instrument was however called *tunava* or *nadi.* Later it was closely associated with Lord Krishna. The association endowed it with mythic dimensions. It is perhaps the only instrument active in all categories of music, namely primitive, folk, art, popular and the devotional. The *Naradiya Shiksha* (600 A.D.) pressed it into service to identify notes employed by reciters of the *sama*s. A very detailed treatment is given to the instrument in the medieval *Sangit Ratnakara* (1247 A.D) in which fifteen varieties of the instrument are dealt with. Five types of fingering techniques, twelve merits and five demerits of blowing and ten chief merits of the player also find place.

The credit of popularizing the present horizontal *bansuri* goes to Pandit Pannalal Ghosh (1911-1960) who brought to it concert status and musical content to match. The two feet long bansuri of Pandit Ghosh was known as *tipperi.*

A player of a *bansuri* holds it in a horizontal position with a slight downward tilt. Both the thumbs are often employed to hold it. Three fingers of the left hand (excluding the little finger) and four fingers of the right hand manipulate the finger holes. The basic playing techniques include covering the sound holes completely, keeping them half-open and cross-fingering. To vary the blowing pressure (especially over-blowing), forms an important aspect of the player's

Batta been

virtuousity.

The vertical *bansuri* has its blowing-end shaped into a narrow opening known as a beak. Near the beak and along the tube is located the edge of the fipple to produce sound. Manipulation of the finger holes yields various notes. The vertical *bansuri* has nearly disappeared from the concert platform though it has not gone into total oblivion. Its high pitch has its uses especially in orchestrated music.

3.2 *Batta been*

- *Vichitra been*
- (H *batta* S *vatuk* = rounded piece of stone used for grinding spices etc. in Indian households; *vichitra* adj. S various, painted)
- *Tata* (See *been*.)

In general appearance similar to the *been*. The fretless *batta-been* has a wooden stem and two gourds below it at both ends. Each gourd (of 45 cms. each) is fitted with screws to the stem. The stem (135 x 20 x 3 cms.) has an ivory bridge at one end covering the complete width. Six playing strings of brass and steel run the whole length and are tied to pegs at the end opposite to the bridge. Twelve sympathetic strings of varying lengths run parallel to and under the playing strings. The *batta been* has two high-pitched side-strings for the *jhala* (>) phase of the musical elaboration.

A prototype of the *batta been* appears to have existed in the medieval *ekatantri vina* (one-stringed lute). However the contemporary version has been credited to Ustad Abdul Aziz Khan of the Patiala court who is said to have invented it in the pre-independence period.

Placing the instrument on the ground the player plucks strings with a steel-wire plectrum worn on the right-hand fingers. A piece of rounded glass (looking like a paper-weight) is held in the left hand to be slid across the strings to produce the required notes.

3.3 *Been*

- *Rudraveena, saraswativeena*
- (n. H S *veena* = lute)

The variant name *rudraveena* suggests the ancient lineage of the instrument in some form. It is believed that the name is traceable to the twelve intervals in the ·octave as they numerically symbolize the twelve *rudra*s, (eleven *rudra*s and one *maha-rudra)* enumerated in Hindu mythology. Sometimes the name *saraswativina* is applied to the been though a majority favours restricting the former name to the

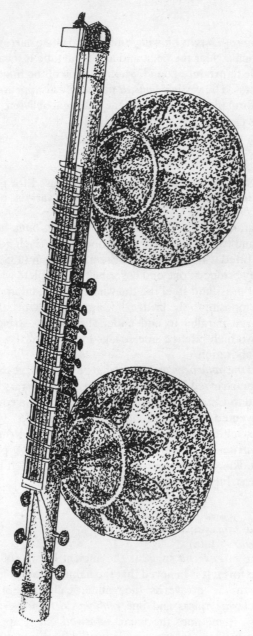

Been

South Indian *vina*.

The *been* has a wide fingerboard of wood (an earlier practice was to use a bamboo for it), with two gourds of 35 cms. each under the stem at both ends. The other important features are: a flat bridge at one end and twenty-four metal frets fixed with wax over the finger board. Four playing strings are supplemented in the *been* by two drone-strings, one on each side.

The ancestry of the *been* goes back to the *kinnari vina* described in great detail by the early musicological texts. The latter is also widely depicted in medieval sculpture. The earliest assignable period of the *kinnari vina* is around 500 A.D. The smaller version of the instrument described as *laghavi* seems to be the direct predecessor of the *been*. Historically, the Mughal Period and especially the reign of Akbar (1542-1605) proved to be the heyday of the *been*. Even today prominent *been* players trace their musical genealogy from Tansen, (1506-1589), the legendary court-musician of Akbar.

The *been* is held in front and across the body in a slanting position with the upper gourd resting on the left shoulder and the lower gourd on the right knee. Playing strings are plucked by the right hand, and the left hand, passing around the stem, presses strings on the frets as required.

3.4 *Dilruba* (adj. P *dil* = heart + *ruba* = attractive)
- *Vitata*

A clear combination of *sitar* and *sarangi*, *dilruba* is a fretted, bowed instrument. On its wooden stem are nineteen, gut-tied, movable and elliptical frets. The bridge at the nether end is placed on a skin-covered, waisted, wooden belly. The four playing strings run over the frets with the eleven sympathetic strings passing underneath. Pegs for the playing strings are at the top while those for the sympathetic strings are at the side. The bow, two feet and a quarter in length, uses black horse-hair. It is held in a grip to ensure forceful bowing.

Held vertically with the lower portion in the lap of the performer, the top of the instrument rests against the left shoulder. The left hand slides over the strings. The frets merely help to locate the positions on the string as per the notes required. The right hand does the bowing.

The instrument seems to be of recent origin. Probably it came into vogue after the *sitar* gained popularity during the early nineteenth century.

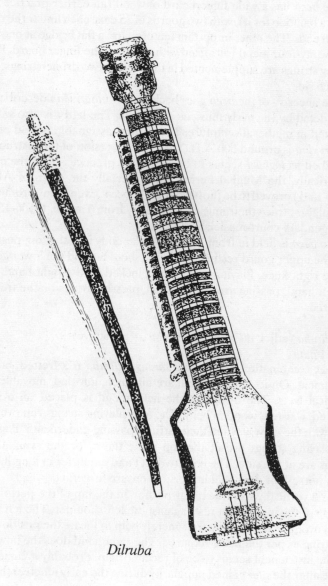

Dilruba

3.5 *Esraj*
● *Vitata*

Very similar to *dilruba* (>) in appearance, playing technique and origin. It has a *sitar*-like stem and the belly of a *sarangi*. However, the *esraj* is rounder in shape and shallow in the middle. Sixteen fixed frets and an equal number of sympathetic strings feature in it. The bow and its use is as in the playing of *dilruba*.

Esraj originated sometime in the early twentieth century and became popular in Bengal. It probably antedated *dilruba*.

It is argued that both *esraj* and *dilruba* were invented as less difficult instruments for the new, amateur music-lovers/performers of the nineteenth century. The amateurs could not be expected to master the traditional, dignified instruments such as the *rudra-vina* etc. and hence the musical concessions to their frailties!

3.6 Harmonium, *baja, samvadini (baja* H *vadya* = that which sounds, *samvadini* = A new term recently coined edging away the English name from which it is loosely derived. Connotes an instrument that employs harmonious notes.)

● *Sushira* is the generally accepted classification. However it is rightly contended that in the harmonium it is the reed which vibrates and not the air-column. The instrument, therefore, needs to be classified differently.

Cabinet or the body is of primary importance in harmonium as it contains all other parts. It is made of wood and the size is determined by the musical requirements such as tonal range, number of reed-lines etc. Rectangular, box-like in shape, the harmonium has two bellows, outer and inner, made of cardboard and glued to the body. The outer bellow may have upto seven folds according to the user's demand. The outer vertical bellow sucks the air into the cabinet and the inner, horizontal bellow presses it into the sound-box. A reed-board with a frame for each of the reeds is fixed on the sound-box. The base of the sound-box is formed by a board *(kisti)* which controls the air-supply to the soundbox. In it are located stoppers.

The harmonium-reeds *(sur)* are individually fixed in wooden frames. Made of brass, the *sur*s are generally obtained in three kinds: *kharaj* (bass), *nar* (male) and *madi* (female) indicating the three timbres. The higher the pitch, the lesser the width, length and thickness of the reed. The three timbres are described as 'lines' and they are available in all the three octaves *(mandra, madhya* and *tara)* custo-

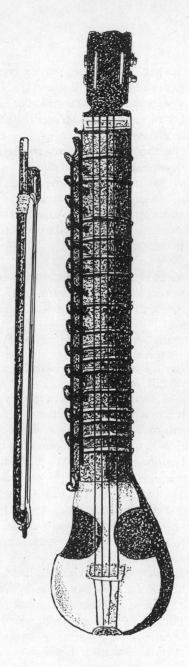

Esraj

Harmonium

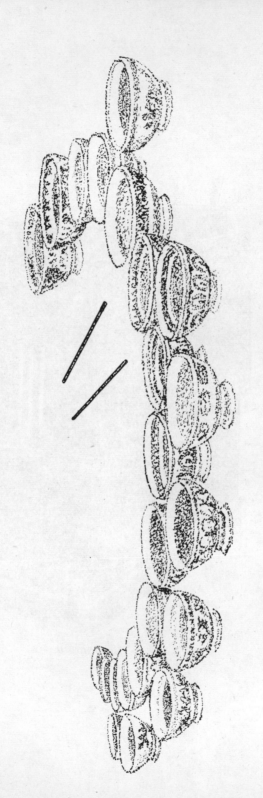

Jaltaranga

marily employed by Indian music-makers. The reeds can be scraped/polished when the *surs* are tuned. The board on which the reeds are arrayed is known as reed-board. Palitana in Saurashtra (Western India) is known for the good quality of reeds manufactured there.

The reed-board/s are joined to another board called *jali* in such a way that the bellow-air, after passing through the reeds can move through separate channels created by the *jali* for each reed.

The operation of the reeds is controlled by two types of keys, namely straight (made of one single piece of wood) and the stick or the English key (made of at least four wooden parts glued together). The keys (white for the major notes such as C, D, E etc. and black for the sharp and flat varieties) number twelve per octave and are fixed on a board from left to right in an ascending order.

The action of the bellow, initiated by the left hand of the player sucks, compresses and pushes the air via sound-box through the reeds. The right-hand fingers of the player presses the keys to allow the desired reeds to vibrate. Harmonium-reeds vibrate freely i.e. the vibrating edges do not touch the frames in which the reeds are fixed.

The instrument, which probably began its Indian career as a pedal-harmonium, soon evolved into the hand-harmonium version. Since then it has evolved further types such as plain, scale- change, folding and portable etc.

The history of the instrument is not clear. It is maintained that Portugese soldiers brought it to India in the seventeenth century. Maharashtra, one of the early centres of the western influence had accepted the pedal-harmonium so well by 1880s that it was freely employed in *keertana,* the religio-musical discourse. It is safe to deduce that the instrument had its first use at least a century prior to the 1880s.

It is customary for the player to sit cross-legged on the platform etc. and keep the instrument in front. Sometimes the instrument partially rests on the lap of the player.

Harmonium being a key-board instrument its tuning takes place at the stage of manufacture.

3.7 *Jalataranga*
- *Jalayantra* (*jala* = water + *taranga* = ripple;*jalayantra* = water instrument, a synonymous name)
- *Ghana.*

Consists of a set of 15 to 24 porcelain (or bronze in early times) bowls

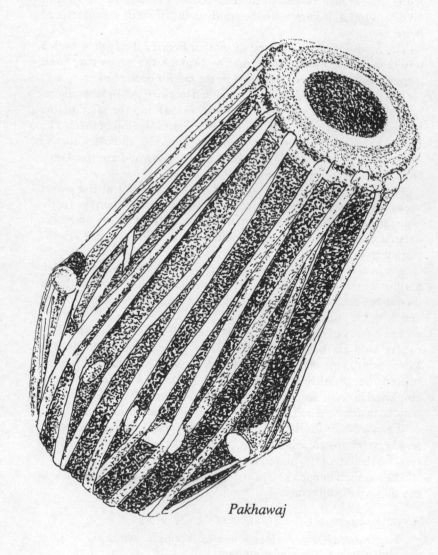

Pakhawaj

of varying sizes and two slender bamboo sticks. Sometimes the tips of the sticks are covered with cotton or wool. The smaller bowls emit higher notes and the larger ones, the lower. Further, more water means lower pitch and less water makes for the higher.

The instrument does not receive a clear mention prior to *Sangit Parijat* (1650) of Ahobala.

The bowls are arranged semi-circular, in front and in easy reach of the player. From left to right the sizes decrease. Having 'tuned' them according to the musical requirements, the artiste plays by striking on the rims of the bowls. The water in the bowls is touched (having hit the bowl) to create special effects. The sticks, one in each hand, encourage quick passages of music and alert playing.

3.8 *Pakhawaj*

- Loosely called *mridanga*.
- Etymological explanations are varied.

(*pakshavadya: paksha* = side + *vadya* = that which sounds; *push-karvadya: pushkara* = a thundering cloud + *vadya;* P *pakh* = *bass* + *awaj* = sound)

- *Avanaddha.*

Bharata in his *Natyashastra* has narrated an engaging story to explain the origin of *mridang,* the prototype of *pakhawaj.* The sage Swati went to Pushkara lake in the rainy season and heard grave and sonorous rhythms of raindrops incessantly falling on lotus-leaves. The sage was thus prompted to create instruments of the *avanaddha* (stretched membranes) category.

A tapering wooden cylinder about 60 cms. in length and 90cms. in diameter in the middle, is carved to have its right and left faces of 16 cms. and 25 cms. diameter, respectively. Both faces of the horizontal drum are covered with goat-skin, though in varying layers. The skin on the right is also thinner. On the right face a mixture of iron-filings, glue, carbon etc. is applied centrally and circular. It is rubbed to high polish and right density to ensure a sonorous and clear tone. The left face gets a coat of a paste made of water, wheat flour, every time afresh prior to a performance. It emits a bass, atonal sound. Membranes can be tightened or loosened by manipulating the leather braces stretching them. Cylindrical wooden blocks inserted between alternate braces and the body also help in this respect. Further, a braid which directly stretches the membranes is struck with a pestle-like device for finer adjustments in tuning.

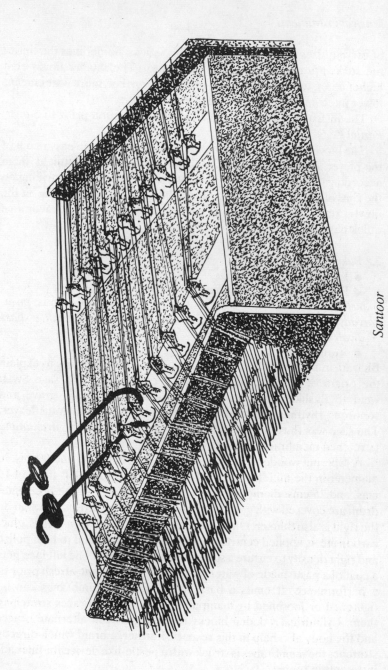

Santoor

Prototypes of the instrument have a very long history. Especially as *mridanga*, the instrument dates back to the great epics, *Ramayana* and *Mahabharata* as well as to the Buddisht texts which refer to it as *muing*. *Natyashastra* of Bharata calls it *pushkara*. It is described as an important drum by Abul Fazl, the perceptive chronicler of Emperor Akbar's times. The medieval texts describe many types of horizontal two-faced drums and deal in great detail in respect of forms of their music.

Players keep the *pakhawaj* on the ground, in front, or take it on the lap. Left hand plays the bass and the right the treble face. The technique relies more on open-palm strokes.

3.9 *Santoor, santir, shatatantri* (*shatatantri* S *shata* = hundred + *tantri* = string)
● *Tata.*
One of the rare dulcimer-type string instruments in the country. It consists of a trapezoid wooden box (60 cms x 30 cms x 3 cms) with fifteen bridges on each side, and four strings on each bridge. Pegs located behind the bridges tighten/loosen the strings. More than one string is allotted to each note and a pair of sticks curved at the striking end, help produce the sound. Generally the instrument has a range of more than two dozen notes.

Some authorities tried to trace the *santoor* back to the ancient *shatatantri vina* or to the *vina* of the Vedic times. The conjectures are not well-supported. It is more likely that this instrument, circulating today in Kashmir, came originally from Central Asia.

The instrument is placed on the ground in front of the player who sits to perform with sticks in both hands.

3.10 *Sarangi, saranga, sarang-vina* (S *saranga* = deer or *saranga* = bow). Sometimes it is derived as *sou* = hundred + *rangi* = colours! Obviously this is eulogy, and not an etymology!
● *Vitata.*
Carved out of one block of wood 60 cms. in height, of adequate width and waisted at the bottom. The lower portion of the block is covered with parchment; the middle with wood to form a finger- board. The top is a box in which are fixed pegs at the right-back and main gut-strings (four). The fretless instrument is played with a horse-hair bow operated by the right hand.

Bowed string-instruments are mentioned in Indian musicological texts from 700 A.D. Medieval references are also plenty. Surprisingly

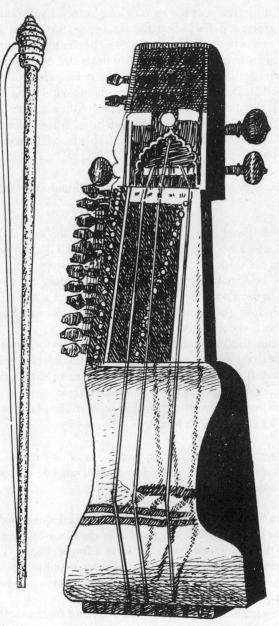

Sarangi

the *sarangi* does not find a place in the Mughal records. On the other hand there are a number of varieties in circulation in Rajasthan and contiguous regions. It is safe to conclude that *sarangi* was for a long time a folk instrument prior to its urban prominence during the late seventeenth century. Its advent as a concert instrument is late, during the last 75 years or so. Till the time, *sarangi* was mostly employed as an accompanying instrument for nautch girls or professional singers.

It is held vertically, with the belly-portion resting on the ground or on the player's lap. The peg-box rests on the right shoulder, the right hand does the bowing and the left the fingering. A special feature of the fingering is that strings are stopped with the back of the finger-nails.

3.11 *Sarod, swarodaya, swaravarta, sarabat*

Attempts have been made to derive the name from *sarada vina* but there is no supporting evidence, as no such instrument is mentioned in musicological texts. Another derivation advocated is *sur + ud,* the latter being the name of a major string instrument from central Asia. *Swarodaya* (S *swara + udaya* (rise of note) or *swaravarta, swara + avarta* (cycle of notes) are obvious cases of Sanskritization in music!)

• *Vitata.*

The fretless, waisted instrument made out of a single block of wood, 1.5 m. in length is similar to *rabab,* an instrument nearly out of vogue. The rounded end (30 cms. in diameter) is covered with parchment, at the centre of which is the bridge. From bridge-end the instrument tapers off towards the neck. The middle portion of the hollow body is covered with a highly polished metal (silver or brass) sheet to from the fingerboard. Six playing strings are supported by twelve sympathetic strings, all of metal. Pegs for the main strings are at the top-end while those for the sympathetic strings are at the side. A smaller and additional metal resonator is screwed at the top-back. A triangular plectrum made of coconut shell is held in the right hand to strum the strings.

Early Indo-Persian literature mentions sarode, *though* musicological texts do not refer to it. Reportedly, Khan Asadulla Khan introduced the instrument in Bengal in the early nineteenth century.

Held in front with a slight slant, the player's left hand slides over the strings and stops them as required. The right hand uses the plectrum.

3.12 *Shehnai, sanai (shehnai. shah* = king + *nai* = pipe)

In Persia a player of *nai* (pipe) pleased the Shah (king) by his artistry

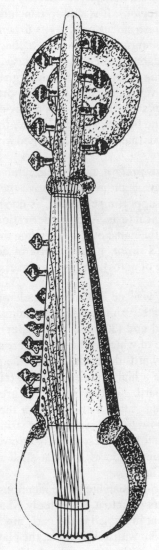

Sarod

Shehnai

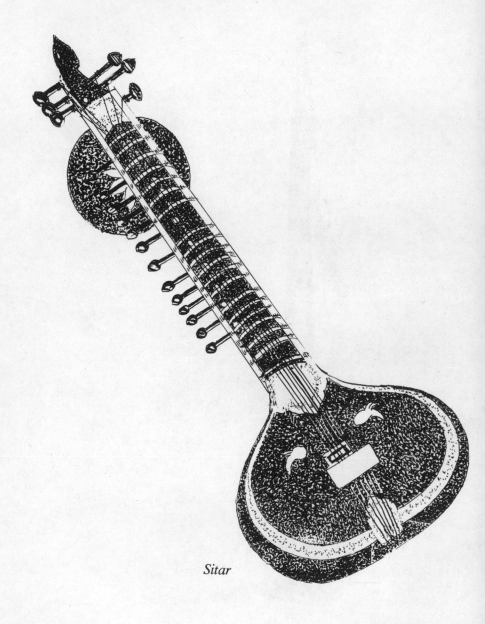

Sitar

and hence the name. Alternatively a player reportedly used a *nai* longer than those in vogue and with better results, thus, bestowing a special status on the instrument.

The double-reed instrument (oboe-like) is a tube made of dark, close-grained, blackwood gradually widening to an end at which a metal bell, shaped as a *dhatura* flower is fixed. At the other end is a reed traditionally made of *pala* grass cultivated in some regions of Uttar Pradesh. Spare reeds and an ivory needle to adjust them are attached to the mouthpiece. There are eight-nine sound holes of which seven are played while others are stopped with wax or kept open at the discretion of the performer. An inevitable accessory is the *sur* or *sruti*, a longer pipe with two or three sound-holes enabling the accompanist to keep a drone.

It is obvious that a prototype of the *shehnai* existed and enjoyed many versions in various parts of the country. Under the generic name *mukhavina*, instruments such as *surnai*, *mohari madhukari*, *tuti*, *naferi* and *sundri* prevailed in Hindustan. Shehnai finds a mention in medieval times and an expert player is listed in *Ain-e-Akbari* (1596-7). *Sangit Parijat* describes in great detail an instrument called *sunadi* that has an ummistakable resemblance to *shehnai*.

The *shehnai* succeeds as a music-maker on account of the skilful opening/closure of the sound-holes and on account of the adroit lip-tongue movements by the player.

3.13 *Sitar, satar* (H S *sapta* = seven + *tar* = string; P *seh* = three + *tar* = string)
- *Tata.*

Legend has Amir Khusro (1310 A.D.) as the inventor.

Satar has a hollow wooden stem made of two strips (34$''$ x 35$''$), the upper concave and the lower hollowed. A wooden and slightly curved disc jointed to the stem at the bottom end covers a gourd cut suitably. The all-important bridge (2 $^3/_4$$''$ x 1 $^1/_4$$''$) flat and of ivory, ebony etc centres the disc. Sometimes a second and a smaller gourd is attached at the top-back for additional resonance. Pegs for seven main strings and eleven sympathetic strings are distributed at the end of the disc. Metal frets, (usually 19) are convex, moveable and traditionally tied with gut.

In spite of claims to the contrary, *sitar* does not seem to have a long history. The Persian *seh-tar*, ancient *tri-tantri vina* and the Kashmiri folk instrument *setar/saitar* have been put forward as prototypes of the in-

Surbahar

strument. Neither Amir Khusro (who is credited to be its inventor) nor Abul Fazl have referred to it. In the eighteenth century it is described as a *nibaddha tambura,* the latter being an instrument similar to *sitar* but prevalent in West Asia.

The player holds the instrument in front, resting the gourd on the ground or on the left in-step. Left hand fingers slide over the frets to stop, stretch or vibrate the strings. A wire plectrum worn on the right forefinger plucks the strings. A plectrum worn over the little finger is employed to play the high pitched side-strings creating drone as well as rhythm.

3.14 *Surbahar, Kacchwa, kacchhapi vina, kashyapi vina* (*Surbahar (sur* = note + *bahar* = delight)
● *Tata.*
A larger edition of the *sitar* (>) in every respect. The flatter gourd resembles a tortoise and sometimes is deliberately made to resemble it through craftsmanship.

The well-known been-player Umrao Khan is credited with the invention of the instrument, a century and a half ago.

The *surbahar* has thicker strings and flatter frets compared to the *sitar* though the playing technique is similar. It is mainly employed for the slow-tempo musical elaborations known as *alapa* (>).

3.15 *Tabla, dayan* (adj. H *dahina* S *dakshin* = right), bayan (adj. H S *vam* = left), *tabla* (A *tabla* = a membranophonic instrument)
● *Avanaddha.*
Mridang/pakhawaj was divided into two in order to create an instrument easier to play.

In reality, *tabla* is a drum-pair in which each drum is to be played by one hand. Usually the bass drum is played by the left hand while the right hand plays the treble. However today *tabla* means the pair as well as the treble-drum.

The treble-drum is carved out of wood (30cms x 17 cms x 20 cms). The bass drum, made of clay or metal is 25 cms. in diameter and tapers off towards the bottom. In both drums the goat-skin membranes (multi-layered in case of the treble drum) have an additional strip round the edges. This ring is fitted in a leather-braid through which pass the braces tied together at the bottom. Tightening or loosening the braces increases or decreases the tension on the membranes. Cylindrical wooden blocks wedged between the braces and the outer walls of the

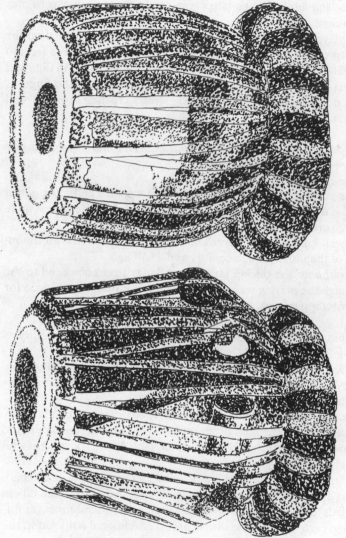

Tabla

treble drum allow finer pitch-adjustments. Pitch-adjustments are also possible through hammer-strokes on the braid. An important feature is the circular and centrally placed coating of iron-filings, carbon etc. on the membrane of the treble drum. It is placed eccentrically on the bass drum.

It is difficult to accept Amir Khusro as the originator of *tabla*. On the other hand the ancient depiction of drums includes a *mridanga* with three component drums, one to be kept on the lap and the other two kept vertically in front, with their faces up. In later centuries the distribution of the drums changed to one vertical and on the lap, and then two horizontal drums placed on the lap, one vertical drum thus getting eliminated in the process. The *Sangit Sar* of Sawai Pratap Sinha describes a variety of *mridanga*, namely, *hudukka*, which came into prominence only in the late eighteenth century.

Both the drums are placed in front of the player who plays the left drum with wrist-pressure and a curved palm with finger tips striking on the membrane. The right drum is played with fingers (facing the membrane).

3.16 *Tanpura, Tambora, tamboora* (P *tumbura,* S *tumba* = a long gourd)
• *Tata*
Tumbaru, the ancient *acharya* (preceptor) of music created it.

The chief features of the *tanpura* are: gourd (70-90 cms in diameter), a hollow pinewood stem, (105-120 cms. in length), a slightly bulging wooden disc covering the vertically cut portion of the gourd and a bridge (of ivory or ebony etc.) centrally placed on the disc. The pegs of the four strings are at the top. A small sound-hole below the bridge ensures resonance. A piece of thread or silk is inserted between strings and the surface of the bridge to create the characteristic resonance of the *tanpura* described as *jawari*. Of the four strings that a traditional *tanpura* has, three are of steel, and the fourth bass string is of brass. Strings are threaded through beads between the bridge and the end-attachment to allow subtler pitch adjustments.

The first unambiguous reference to the *tanpura* is in *Sangit Parijat* (1650). It is neither mentioned by the earlier texts nor does it find a place in sculptures. According to some authorities a functional prototype of the *tambora* is the *tritantri vina* of the medieval times. Abul Fazl describes an instrument called *swaravina* specifying it however as a *been* (>) without frets. *Sangit Samay Sar* (1250 A.D.) refers to it. It

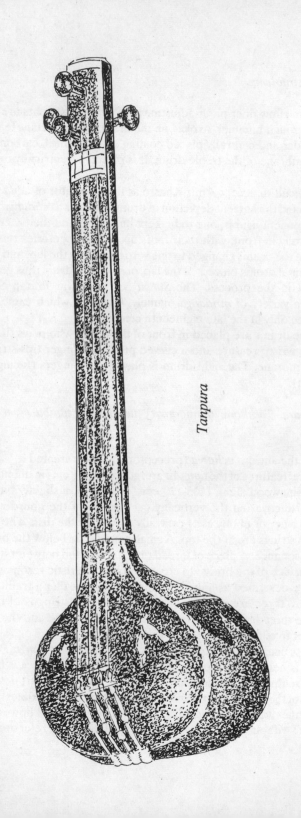

Tanpura

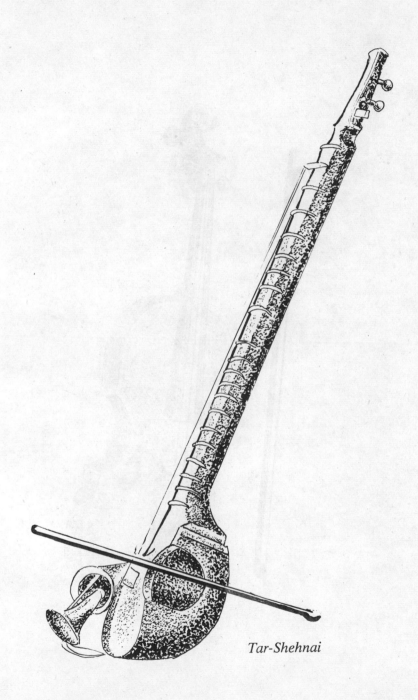

Tar-Shehnai

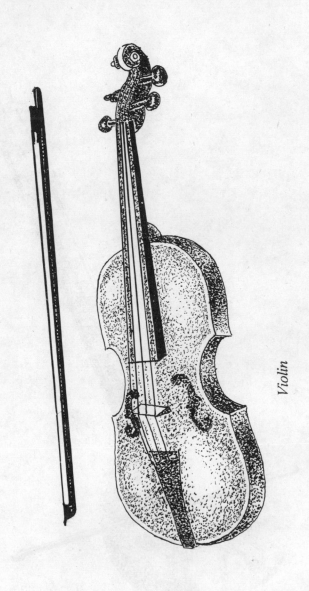

Violin

is also important to note that *tamburi,* a four-stringed, one piece drone used by non-elite musicians could easily claim to be a prototype of the *tanpura.*

The traditional position to play the drone instrument is to hold it upright, the player taking it on the lap or keeping the gourd on the ground and adopting a suitable sitting posture. To hold it horizontal in front while sitting in a crossed-legged position is, though convenient, not approved by tradition.

To play the *tanpura,* strings are strummed from left to right in sequence and succession. The first string is played by the third finger of the right hand, the remaining three being played by the forefinger.

3.17 *Tar-shehnai (tar* = string + *shehnai)*
● *Tata*

It is, virtually speaking, an *esraj* with a gramophone sound-box and a small megaphone attached to the resonator. Of very recent origin, its tone has a similarity with that of the *shehnai* in addition to the capacity to produce a continuous sound of a string instrument. The apparently confusing name has therefore a justification!

3.18 *Violin*

An obvious and a successful transplant from the West, the bowed string instrument is well established on the Hindustani concert stage at least from 1885.

Played in a sitting position and without the use of a chin-rest the Indian playing style intrigued the non-Indian observers of the scene.

During the last hundred years two kinds of playing techiques have crystallized. One called *gatkari* and the other Carnatic, though the latter is also being employed to render Hindustani music. The former is conducive for a rhythm-oriented and virile expression, while the latter encourages sustained, melodic production of sound.

Bibliography

Naradiya Shiksha, Narada (4th century A.D.), critically edited with translations and explanatory notes by Ms Usha Bhise, Bhandarkar Oriental Research Institute, Pune, 1986.

Dattilam, Dattila (4th century B.C.), edited by Sambasiva Shastri, Trivandrum Government Press, 1930.

Chatvarinshatnag nirupanam, Narada (4th century B.C.), edited by B. C. Sukthankar, Bombay, 1914.

Bruhaddeshi, Matangmuni (6th or 9th century A.D.), edited by Sambasiva Shastri, 1928.

Bharatbhashyam, Nanyabhupal (1097-1133), edited by Chaitanya Desai, Khairagarh, 1961.

Sangeetsamayasara, Parshvadev (1165), edited by Ganapati Shastri, Trivandrum Government Press, 1925.

Varna Ratnakara, Jyotireshwara (1280-1340), edited by S. K. Sen, Asiatic Society of Bengal, Calcutta, 1940.

Ghunyat-Ul-Munya, author not known (1374-75), under the patronage of Malik Shamsuddin Ibrahim Hasan Abu Raja, the Naib of Gujrat (1374-1377), Persian, edited by Sarmadee Shahab, Asia Publishing House, Bombay, 1978.

Sangeet Raj, Maharana Kumbh (1433-1468), King of Chittorgarh (Rajasthan), Sanskrit, edited by Premalata Sharma, Varanasi Hindu Vishvavidyalaya, 1963.

Mansingh aur Mankutuhal (1486 approx.), Dwivedi Hariharniwas, Gwalior, Vidyamandir Prakashan, 1954.

Sangeet Damodar, Shubhankara (15th century), Bengal, Sanskrit, edited by Gaurinath, Calcutta, Sanskrit College, 1960.

Sahasrasa, Nayak Bakhshu (1501-1537), Gwalior, under the patronage of Raja Mansingh, edited by Premlata Sharma, Sangeet Natak Akademi, 1972.

Babarnama, Jahiruddin Babar (1530), translated into Hindi by Yughit Naval Puri, New Delhi, Sahitya Akademi, 1974.

Swaramelkalanidhi, Ramamatya (1550), Vijay Nagar, Shree Ganesh Press, 1910.

Ragmanjiri, Pundarik Vitthal (1556-1605), edited by B. S. Sukthankar, Aryabhushan Press, 1918.

Sadragchandrodaya, Pundarik Vitthal (1556-1605), edited by Ganesh Vajratank, Bombay, Nirnaysagar, 1912.

Rasakaumudi, Shrikantha (1575), a brahmin from South India, worked for the king of Navanagar (Porbander), Sanskrit, edited by B. J. Sandesara, Oriental Institute, Baroda, 1963.

Kitab-I-Nauras, Ibrahim Adilshah II (1580-1627), Bijapur, Persian, edited by Nazir Ahmed, Bharatiya Kala Kendra, 1956.

Ain-i-Akbari, Shaykh Abu 'I' Fazal (1590), edited by S. L. Goomer, New Delhi, Naresh Jain (publisher), 1965.

Ragvibodh, Somnath (1610), Andhra Pradesh, Bombay, edited by B. S. Sukthankar, 1911.

Sangeet Parijat, Ahobal Pandit (1620), Dhanwad State, translated by Kalind-Hathras, Sangeet Karyalaya, 1971.

Sangeet Darpan, Damodar (1625), translated by Vishvambhar Bhatt Hathras, Sangeet Karyalaya, 1971.

Ragtatvavibodh, Shreenivas Pandit (1650-1680), edited by B. S. Sukthankar, Bombay, Aryabhushan Press, 1918.

Anup Sangeet Vilas, Bhavabhatta (1650-1709), Dhavalpur (in Abhir State), Bombay, edited by B. S. Sukthankar, 1921.

Hridaykautukam & Hriday Prakash, Hridaynarayan (1667), Gadha (Jabalpur), Bombay, edited by B. S. Sukthankar, 1918.

Ragtarangini, Lochana (1675), edited by B. S. Sukthankar, Bombay, Aryabhushan Press, 1918.

Sangeetsaramrita, King Tulja (1729-1735), Tanjore, Sanskrit, Bombay, Nirnaysagar, 1911.

On Musical Modes of the Hindus, *Music of India*, Jones William (1779), Calcutta, Gupta.

A Treatise on the Music of India, Augustus Willard, Calcutta, 1834, Sunil Gupta, 1962.

Sangeet-Rag-Kalpadrum, Vyas Krishnanand, 1842.

Kanun Sitar, Sadik Ali (after 1853).

Muladhar Vol. I & II, Kelvade Meenappa Vyankappa, Bombay, Nirnaysagar, 1907.

Sangeet Darpan Masik Pustak, Ichalkaranjikar Balkrishnabuwa, Bombay, 1975.

Six Principal Ragas with Brief View of Hindu Music, 1877, Tagore Sourindro, Neeraj Publications, 1982.

Samay-i-Isharat (Lit. Capital Stock of Bliss, commonly known as Laws of Music — Hindustani), Delhi, Narayani Press, 1286AH, 1881 A.D.

Sangeet Swaraprakash I, Abdul Karim Khan (1884-1937), Belgaum, 1911.

Hindustani Music and the Gayan Samaj, Pune, Gayan Samaj Office, 1887.

The Music and Musical Instruments of Southern India and Deccan, Day C. R., London, 1891.

Navaratnabhashya tatha Rasvilas, Shukla Krishnabihari, Bombay, Khemraj Shrikrishnadas, 1893.

Shree Sangeet-Kaladhar, Dahyalal Shivram (end of 19th century), Gujarati, Bhavnagar, Channalal Dahyalal Nayak, 1938.

Ragvilas, Malwe Anant Sakharam, Bombay, 1905.

Inayat-Geet-Ratnavali, Inayat Khan Rehmat Khan Pathan, 1903, Bombay.

Gayansamaj Pustakmala, Banahatti N. D., Pune, Gayan Samaj, 1906.

Ragvibodh Praveshika, B. S. Sukthankar, Bombay Nirnaysagar Press, 1911.

Contribution to the Study of Ancient Hindu Music, Bhandarkar Prabhakar, Bombay, British India Press, 1912.

Introduction to the Study of Music, Clements E., Allahabad, Kitab Mahal, 1912.

The Music of Hindustan, Strangways A. H. Fox, Oxford, Clarendon Press, 1914.

Ganasopan, Gulabraomaharaj, 1914.

Theory of Indian Music as expounded by Somnatha, Deval K. B., Poona, Aryabhushan, 1916.

Sangeetshastra, Shukla Nathuram Sundarji, Gujrati, 1918.

The Ragas of Hindustan, Deval K. B., Poona, The Philharmonic Society of Western India, 1918.

The Ragas of Hindustan Vol. I & II, The Phiharmonic Society of Western India, Poona, Aryabhushan Press, 1918.

Abhinavtalmanjiri, Kashinath Apatulsi, (-1920), edited by Vishnu Narayan Bhatkhande, Bombay, Nirnaysagar Press, 1914.

The Music of India, 1921, Popley H. A., New Delhi, Y. M. C. A. Publication, 1966 (Third Edition).

Git Sutra-Sar (translator's explanation and notes on grammar and theory of Hindustani music as spoken of in Bengali), Bannerji Himanshu S., 1925.

Rag Pravesh Lalit, Paluskar Vishnu Digambar, Nasik, Sangeet Printing Press, 1927.

Rag Pravesh Bhag 19, (Rag-Sorath-Desh), Paluskar Vishnu Digambar, Nasik Sangeet Printing Press, 1929.

Gavaiyonka Jahaj, Manohar Pustakalaya, Mathura, 1939.

Gavaiyonka Mela, Manohar Pustakalaya, Mathura, 1939.

Padya Mimamsa, Sahasrabuddhe V. J., Kolhapur, G. V. Kulkarni, 1941.

Sangeet Sudha Sagar, Chattopadhyaya (Panubabu), Bengali, Banaras, Nripendrakrishna Chattopadhyay, 1941.

Marathi Chhandashastra (Nibandh), Patwardhan Govind Vishnu Khasgivale), Miraj, 1947.

Ragas and Raginis, Sanyal Amiya Nath, Calcutta, Orient Longmans, 1959.

Amir Khusrau's Contribution to the Indus-Muslim Music, S. Qudratullah Fatimi, Islamabad, Pakistan National Council of the Arts, 1975.

Ashtacchapiya Bhakti Sangeet: Udbhav aur Vikas I, II, III, Nayak C. C., Ahmedabad, 1983.

Index

Key to pronunciation :

अ	a	च	ch
आ	ah	छ	chh
इ	i	ज	j
ई	ee	झ	jh
उ	u	ञ	yn
ऊ	oo	ट	t(t)
ए	e	ठ	t(t)h
ऐ	ai	ड	d(d)
ओ	o	ढ	d(d)h
औ	ou	ण	n(n)
अं	am/an depending on the following consonant	त	t
		थ	th
		द	d
अनुस्वार	the nasanlization is denoted by (n)	ध	dh
		न	n
अ:	aha	प	p
ऋ	ru	फ	ph
ॠ	roo	ब	b
क	k	भ	bh
ख	kh	म	m
ग	g	य	y
घ	gh	र	r
ङ	ng	ल	l

व	v	ह	h
श	sh	ळ	l(l)
ष	sh(h)	क्ष	ksh
स	s	ज्ञ	jn

Note:

1. The spelling in vogue is normally used in the text. However, the Devnagri version and its correct pronunciation are given in the index at the end of the book. Diacritical signs are intentionally avoided and a logical system has been specially devised in view of the nature of Hindi, Sanskrit, Persian and Arabic words.

2. The hyphen – is used at times to denote the syllables as in *sha-hanah-ee.*

Abhijata	अभिजात	Abhijahta	2.1
Abhog	आभोग	Ahbhog	1.5.10, 2.33
Abhyasa	अभ्यास	Abhyahsa	2.12
Acchop	अछोप	Achhop	2.3
Achala	अचल	Achala	2.2
Achetan	अचेतन	Achetan	2.118
Ad	आड	Ahd	2.4
Ad-bansuri	अड-बांसुरी	Ad-bah(n)suri	3.1
Adhama	अधम	Adhama	2.5
Adhar shikha	अधर शिखा	Adharashikhah	2.130
Ad paran	आड-परन	Ahd paran	1.6.13
Ahata	आहत	Ah-hat	2.6, 2.32, 2,78
Akal tihai	अकाल तिहाई	Akahl tihah-ee	1.6.4
Akhada	अखाडा	Akhahdah	1.5.14
Alankara	अलंकार	Alankahra	2.7
Alap	आलाप	Ahlahpa	1.5.15, 2.8
Alapapradhan	आलापप्रधान	Ahlahpapradhahn	2.96
Algooz	अल्गूज	Algooz	3.1
Alpatva	अल्पत्त्व	Alpatva	2.12
Am raga	आम राग	Ahm rahga	2.96
Amukta	अमुक्त	Amukta	2.9

Atikranta	अतिक्रान्त	Atikrahnta	2.70
Ati sukshma	अति सूक्ष्म	Ati sookshma	2.78
Atitagraha	अतीतग्रह	Ateetagraha	2.125
Atit paran	अतीत परन	Ateet paran	1.6.13
Atodya	आतोद्य	Ahtodya	2.144
Auchar	औचार	Auchahr	2.8
Avarta /na	आवर्त / न	Ahvarta /na	2.15
Avaroha	अवरोह	Avaroha	2.7, 2.147
Avanaddha	अवनद्ध	Avanaddha	2.14, 2.144
Avikrit	अविकृत	Avikrut	2.2

B

Bada khayal	बडा ख्याल	Bad(d)ah khyahl	1.5.15
Baddi	बद्दी	Baddi	2.14, 2.144
Badhat	बढत	Badhata	1.5.15, 2.16
Bahirgeet	बहिर्गीत	Bahirgeet	2.84
Bahutva	बहुत्व	Bahutva	2.18, 2.12
Baj	बाज	Bahj	2.19
Baja	बाजा	Bahjah	3.6
Bajant	बजंत	Bajanta	2.89
Bajki tar	बाजकी तार	Bahjki tahr	2.19, 2.130
Bajana	बजाना	Bajahnah	1.3.2
Bajavaiyya	बजवैय्या	Bajavaiyyah	1.3.2
Baithak	बैठक	Bait(t)hak	1.1
Baithana	बैठना	Bait(t)hanah	1.1
Bal	बल	Bal	1.6.15
Bandhan	बन्धान	Bandhahn	2.8
Bandish	बंदिश	Bandish	1.5.2
Bandishki thumri	बंदिशकी ठुमरी	Bandishki t(t)humri	1.5.28
Bani	बानी	Bahni	1.5.10
Bansari	बांसरी	Bahnsari	3.1
Bansuri	बांसुरी	Bahnsuri	3.1
Bant	बांट	Bant(t)	2.20

Barabar	बराबर	Barahbar	2.17
Barabari gat	बराबरी गत	Barahbari gat	1.6.4
Baradasta	बरदस्ता	Bardastah	1.5.14
Barasi	बरसी	Barasi	1.1.2
Batme bol	बातमें बोल	Bahtme bol	1.5.28
Batta been	बट्टा बीन	Bat(t)t(t)ah been	3.2
Bayan	बायाँ	Bayah(n)	3.15
Bedam paran	बेदम परन	Bedam paran	1.6.13
Been	बीन	Been	3.3
Behalva	बेहलावा	Behalahvah	2.7
Beher	बेहेर	Beher	1.5.12
Bemancha	बेमंचा	Bemanchah	2.21
Bhagna	भग्न	Bhagna	2.110
Bhajan	भजन	Bhajan	1.5.3
Bhanda	भांडा	Bhahnd(d)ah	2.14
Bhari	भरी	Bhari	2.125
Bhavak	भावक	Bhahvak	1.3.7
Bina dha paran	बिना धा परन	Binah dhah paran	1.6.13
Bina kiti paran	बिना किटी परन	Binah kit(t)i paran	1.6.13
Biruda	बिरूद	Biruda	1.5.3
Birudawali paran	बिरूदावली परन	Birudahwahli paran	1.6.13
Bol	बोल	Bol	1.5.15, 1.6.1, 2.125
Bol-alap	बोल–आलाप	Bol-ahlahp	1.5.15
Bol-banav	बोल बनाव	Bol banahv	1.5.28
Bol-bant	बोल बाँट	Bol bahnt(t)	1.5.28
Bol-lay/a	बोल लय	Bol-lay/a	1.5.15
Bolme bat	बोलमें बात	Bolme(n) baht(t)	1.5.28
Bol-tan	बोल तान	Boltahn	1.5.15
Budhwa mangal	बुढवा मंगल	Bud(d)hvah mangal	1.1.9
Bulbul tarang	बुल्बुल तरंग	Bulbul tarang	1.5.18
Bund	बंद	Band	2.53
Buzurg	बुजुर्ग	Bujurg	1.3.3

'C'

Chabi	चाबी	Chahbi	2.14, 2.117
Chaddar	चद्दर	Chaddar	2.14
Chadha	चढा	Chad(d)ha	2.111
Chakradar	चक्रदार	Chakradahr	1.6.4, 1.6.13
Chaiti	चैती	Chaitee	1.5.5
Chal	चाल	Chahl	2.23
Chala	चल	Chal	2.2
Chalan	चलन	Chalan	2.22
Chhalika	छलिक	Chhalika	1.5.28
Chapak	चपक	Chapak	2.24
Chaturmukha	चतुर्मुख	Chaturmukha	1.5.4
Chaturanga	चतुरंग	Chaturanga	1.5.4
Chatursa	चतुस्र	Chatusra	2.61, 2.125
Chaukhat	चौखट	Chaukhat(t)	2.34
Chang	चंग	Chang	1.5.14
Charan	चरण	Charan(n)	1.5.3, 2.88
Chibuk	चिबुक	Chibuk	2.130
Cheez	चीझ	Cheej	1.5.6
Chehal	चेहाल	Che-hahl	2.111
Chetan	चेतन	Chetan	2.118
Chhalla	छल्ला	Chhallah	2.14, 2.34
Chhanda	छंद	Chhanda	2.25
Chhaviman	छविमान	Chhavimahn	2.111
Chhayalaga	छायाल्ग	Chhahyahlaga	2.96
Chhed	छेड	Ched(d)	1.6.2
Chhavi paran	छवि परन	Chhavi paran	1.6.13
Chhoot	छूट	Chhoot(t)	2.26
Chhota khayal	छोटा ख्याल	Chhotah khyahl	1.5.15
Chhutkar paran	छुटकर परन	Chhut(t)kar paran	1.6.13
Chhutput paran	छुटपुट् परन	Chhut(t)put(t) paran	1.6.13
Chikari	चिकारी	Chikahri	2.130
Chipli	चिपळी	Chipl(l)i	1.5.3
Chitravritti	चित्रवृत्ति	Chitravrutti	2.141, 2.151

Dhruvaka	धृवक	Dhruvaka	2.30
Dhruva prabandha	धृव प्रबंध	Dhruva prabandha	1.5.10
Dhumkit baj	धुमकिट बाज	Dhumakit(t)a bahj	2.29
Dhun	धुन	Dhun	1.6.3
Dhun-raga	धुन राग	Dhun-rahga	2.96
Dhuya	धुया	Dhuyah	2.8
Dilruba	दिलरूबा	Dilrubah	3.4
Dimdi	दिमडी	Dimd(d)ee	1.5.3
Doha	दोहा	Dohah	1.5.9
Dolak	दोलक	Dolak	2.34
Dombika-gayan	डोंबिका-गायन	D(d)ombikah-gahyan	1.5.28
Dora	दोरा	Dora	1.6.15
Dori	दोरी	Dori	2.34
Druta	द्रुत	Druta	2.31, 2.60
Drut khayal	द्रुत ख्याल	Druta khayahl	1.5.15
Dugun	दुगुन	Dugun	1.5.28
Duguni gat	दुगुनी गत	Duguni gat	1.6.4
Du-hatti paran	दु-हत्ती परन	Du-hatti paran	1.6.13
Dumukhi gat	दुमुखी गत	Dumukhi gat	1.6.4
Dwipad	द्विपद	Dwipad	1.5.9

'E'

Ek-hatti paran	एक-हत्ती परन	Ek-hatti paran	1.6.13
Ekala	एकल	Ekala	1.2.1
Ekamatrika	एक मात्रिक	Ekamahtrik	2.56
Ektantri vina	एकतंत्री वीणा	Ektantri veen(n)ah	3.2
Esraj	इसराज	Esrahj	3.5

'F'

Farad gat	फरद गत	Farad gat	1.6.4
Farmaishi paran	फर्माइशी परन	Farmah-ishee paran	1.6.13

'G'

Gadha	गाढ	Gahd(d)ha	2.111
Gaj	गज	Gaj	2.130
Gajra	गजरा	Gajarah	2.14
Gamaka	गमक	Gamak	2.32
Gambhir	गंभीर	Gambheer	2.111
Gana	गान	Gahna	2.33
Gandhar bani	गांधार बानी	Gahndhahr bahnee	2.8
Ganewala	गानेवाला	Gahnevahlah	1.3.7
Ganewali	गानेवाली	Gahnevahlee	1.3.7
Gandhar	गंधार	Gandhahr	2.108
Gandharva	गांधर्व	Gahndharva	2.33
Gandharva	गंधर्व	Gandharva	1.3.6
Ganika	गणिका	Gan(n)ikah	1.1
Gardan	गर्दन	Gardan	2.130
Gat	गत	Gat	1.6.4
Gathika	गाथिक	Gahthika	2.126
Gatkari	गतकारी	Gatakahri	3.18
Gat paran	गत-परन	Gat paran	1.6.4
Gatta	गट्टा	Gat(t)t(t)ah	2.14
Gat-toda	गत-तोडा	Gat-tod(d)ah	1.6.4
Gavaiyya	गवैय्या	Gavaiyyah	1.3.8
Gayaka	गायक	Gahyak	1.3.7
Gayika	गायिका	Gayikah	1.3.7
Geet	गीत	Geet	1.5.11
Geya	गेय	Geya	2.145
Ghada	घडा	Ghad(d)ah	2.14
Ghana	घन	Ghana	2.111, 2.34, 2.144
Ghar	घर	Ghar	2.14
Gharana	घराना	Gharahnah	2.35
Ghasit	घसीट	Ghaseet(t)	2.36
Ghat	घट	Ghat(t)	2.14, 2.130
Ghazal	गझल	Gazal	1.5.12
Ghera	घेरा	Gherah	2.14

Ghodi	घोडी	Ghod(d)ee	2.130
Ghudach	घुडच	Ghud(d)ach	2.130
Ghundi	घुंडी	Ghund(d)ee	2.14, 2.34
Ghungroo	घुंगरू	Ghungarooh	2.34
Gitanuga	गीतानुग	Geetahnuga	Preface 3
Gitakari	गिटकरी	Git(t)akari	1.5.27, 2.52
Gittak	गिट्टक	Git(t)t(t)ak	2.14
Gol	गोल	Gol	2.34
Goli	गोली	Golee	2.34
Gopuccha yati	गोपुच्छ यति	Gopuchha yati	2.125
Gopuccha paran	गोपुच्छ परन	Gopuchha paran	1.6.13
Goshthi	गोष्ठी	Goshthee	1.1
Gounharin	गौनहारिन	Gounhahrin	1.5.14
Graha	ग्रह	Graha	2.37, 2.125
Sama graha	सम ग्रह	Sama graha	2.37, 2.125
Atita graha	अतीत ग्रह	Ateeta graha	2.37, 2.125
Anagata graha	अनागत ग्रह	Anahgata graha	2.37, 2.25
Vishama graha	विषम ग्रह	Vishama graha	2.37, 2.125
Gulu	गुलु	Gulu	2.130
Gumphita	गुम्फित	Gumphita	2.32
Guna	गुण	Gun(n)a	2.38
Gunakara	गुणकार	Gun(n)akahra	1.3.9
Guni	गुनी	Guni	1.3.9
Guru	गुरू	Guru	2.39, 2.60, 2.67
Guru-shishya parampara	गुरू-शिष्य-परंपरा	Guru-shishya paramparah	Preface

'H'

Halki	हलकी	Halkee	2.111
Harmonium	हार्मोनियम	Hahrmoniyam	3.6
Hathiko rokna paran	हाथी को रोकना परन	Hahthiko roknah paran	1.6.13
Hathiko nachana paran	हाथी को नचाना परन	Hathiko nachah-nah paran	

Hathoudi	हथौडि	Hathaud(d)i	2.34
Hazari	हाजरी	Hahjree	1.2.4
Holi	होलि	Holi	1.5.13
Hori	होरी	Horee	1.5.13
Husn-e-matla	हुस्न-ए-मतला	Husna-e-matlah	1.5.12

'I'

| Indavi | इंदवी | Indavee | 2.14 |

'J'

Jabadi	जबडी	Jabad(d)ee	2.126
Jagahki paran	जगहकी परन	Jaga-hakee paran	1.6.13
Jai shabdaki paran	जय शब्द की परन	Jay shabdakee paran	1.6.13
Jalatarang	जलतरंग	Jalataranga	3.7
Jalayantra	जलयंत्र	Jalayantra	3.7
Jali	जालि	Jahli	3.6
Jamjama	जमजमा	Jamjamah	1.5.27, 2.40
Janak raga	जनक राग	Janak rahga	2.135
Janya (raga)	जन्य	Jannya rahga	2.135
Jarab	जरब	Jarab	2.41
Jati	जाति	Jahti	2.125, 2.147
Jawa	जवा	Javah	2.130
Jawab	जवाब	Javahb	2.42
Jawabi paran	जवाबी परन	Javahbee paran	1.6.13
Jawari	जवारी	Javahree	2.43, 2.130
Jawaridar	जवारीदार	Javahreedahr	2.111, 2.130
Jhala	झाला	Jhahlah	1.6.5, 2.8
Jhalkutiya	झल्कुटिया	Jhalkut(t)iyah	1.5.5
Jhampangi paran	झंपांगी परन	Jhampah(n)gee paran	1.6.13
Jhanj	झांज	jhahnj	1.5.3, 2.14
Jhardar	झारदार	Jhahrdahr	2.111, 2.130

Jhatka	झटका	Jhat(t)kah	2.44
Jhilli	झिल्ली	Jhillee	2.14
Jhoolna paran	झूलना परन	Jhoolnah paran	1.6.13
Jhumri	झुमरी	Jhumree	1.5.28
Jila	जिला	Jhilah	2.45
Jiwa	जिवा	Jivah	2.43
Jod	जोड	Jod(d)	2.8
Jod gat	जोड गत	Jod(d) gat	1.6.4
Jodki tar	जोड की तार	Jod(d)kee tahr	2.130
Jodka paran	जोडका परन	Jod(d)kah paran	1.6.13
Jod-nawaz	जोडनवाझ	Jod(d) nawaz	2.46
Jugalbandi	जुगलबंदी	Jugalbandee	1.2.2

'K'

Kacchapi vina	कच्छपी वीणा	Kacchapee veen(n)ah	3.14
Kacchwa	कछवा	Kachhavah	3.14
Kada	कडा	Kad(d)ah	2.14
Kadak bijli paran	कडक बिजली परन	Kadak bijlee paran	1.6.13
Kaddu	कद्दू	Kaddoo	2.130
Kaki	काकी	Kahkee	2.126
Kakoli	काकोली	Kahkolee	2.110
Kafiya	काफिया	Kahfiyah	1.5.12
Kajli	कजली	Kajlee	1.5.14
Kajri	कजरी	Kajree	1.5.14
Kaku	काकु	Kahku	2.47
Kakubha	ककुभ	Kakubha	2.130
Kala	काल	Kahla	2.125
Kala	कला	Kalah	2.125
Kalakar	कलाकार	Kalahkahr	1.3.11
Kalash	कलश	Kalash	2.117
Kalavan	कलावान	Kalahvahn	1.3.10
Kalavant	कलावंत	Kalahvant	1.3.10

Khayal-numa	ख्याल नुमा	Khyahl numah	1.5.25
Khod	खोड	Khod(d)	2.14
Khula-bund	खुला-बंद	Khulah band	2.53
Khuli	खुली	Khulee	2.126
Khunti	खुंटी	Khunt(t)ee	2.130
Khyaliya	ख्यालिया	Khyahliyah	1.3.12
Kinar	किनार	Kinahr	2.14
Kinnari vina	किन्नरी वीणा	Kinnaree veena	3.3
Kisti	किस्ती	Kistee	3.6
Kolahala	कोलाहल	Kolahhal	2.78
Komala	कोमल	Komal	2.111
Kon	कोन	Kon	2.130
Kothiwale	कोठीवाले	Kot(t)hivahle	1.5.2
Krama	क्रम	Krama	2.54
Krintana	क्रिन्तन	Krintana	2.55
Krisha	कृश	Krusha	2.110
Kritrim	कृत्रिम	Krutrim	2.78
Kriya	क्रिया	Kriyah	2.125
Kuad	कुआड	Ku-ahd(d)	2.4, 2.60
Kuta	कूट	Koot(t)	2.126
Kuttikara	कुड्डिकार	Kut(t)t(t)ikahr	1.5.11

'L'

Lachau	लचाऊ	Lacha-oo	1.5.28
Lad gutthi	लड गुत्थी	Lad(d) gutthee	1.6.7, 2.8
Lad lapet	लड लपेट	Lad(d) lapet(t)	1.6.8, 2.8
Ladi	लडी	Lad(d)ee	1.6.6, 2.8
Laggi	लग्गी	Laggee	1.6.9
Laghavi	लाघवी	Lahghavee	3.3
Laghu	लघु	Laghu	2.56, 2.60, 2.67
Lakadi	लकडी	Lakad(d)ee	1.5.14, 2.14
Lakshana	लक्षण	Lakshan(n)a	1.5.16, 2.57
Lakshangeet	लक्षणगीत	Lakshan(n)geet	1.5.16

Margi	मार्गी	Mahrgee	2.65
Masala	मसाला	Masahlah	2.14
Masitkhani gat	मसीतखानी गत	Maseetkhahnee gat	1.6.4
Matha	माठा	Maht(t)hah	2.8
Mata	मत	Mata	2.66
Matla	मतला	Matalah	1.5.12
Matra	मात्रा	Mahtrah	2.60, 2.67
Matu	मातु	Mahtu	2.68, 2.145
Matukara	मातुकार	Mahtukahr	1.5.11
Meend	मींड	Meend	2.70
Mela	मेल	Mela	2.71, 2.135
Mela	मेला	Melah	1.2.7
Melakarta	मेलकर्ता	Melakartah	2.72, 2.135
Melapaka	मेलापक	Melahpaka	2.33
Mehfil	मेहफिल	Mehfil	1.1.6
Meru	मेरू	Meroo	2.130
Mijrab	मिजराब	Mijrahb	2.130
Mirashi	मिराशी	**Mirahshee**	1.3.13
Mirasin	मिरासिन	Mirahsin	1.3.13
Misal	मिसाल	Misahl	2.69
Mishra	मिश्र	Mishra	2.61, 2.73,
			2.118, 2.125
Mishra raga	मिश्र राग	Mishra rahga	2.96
Misra	मिसरा	Misrah	1.5.12
Mohara	मोहरा	Mohrah	1.6.10
Mohari	मोहरी	Mohree	3.12
Mooth	मूठ	Moot(t)h	2.130
Mridang	मृदंग	Mruda(n)ga	3.8
Mrishta	मृष्ट	Mrusht(t)ha	2.111
Mukh	मुख	Mukh	1.6.15, 2.14
Mudra	मुद्रा	Mudrah	1.5.3, 2.74
Mudrita	मुद्रित	Mudrita	2.32
Mukam	मुकाम	Mukahm	2.71
Mukh	मुख	Mukh	1.6.15, 2.14

Mukha	मुख	Mukha	2.75, 2.117
Mukhda	मुखडा	Mukhad(d)ah	1.5.15, 1.6.10, 1.6.11, 2.75
Mukh-patti	मुखपत्ती	Mukhapattee	2.117
Mukhari	मुखरी	Mukharee	2.76
Mukhvina	मुखवीणा	Mukhaveen(n)ah	3.12
Mukta	मुक्त	Mukta	2.9
Murali	मुरलि	Murali	3.1
Murchhana	मूर्च्छना	Moorchhanah	2.77, 2.126
Murki	मुरकी	Murkee	1.5.27, 2.52
Mushaira	मुशायरा	Mushahyrah	1.5.12

'N'

Nabhi	नाभी	Nahbhee	2.117, 2.130
Nachka paran	नाचका परन	Nahchkah paran	1.6.13
Nada	नाद	Nahda	2.78
Nada-chhidra	नाद छिद्र	Nahd chhidra	2.117
Nadi	नाडी	Nahd(d)ee	3.1
Naferi	नफेरी	Napheree	3.12
Nagaraka	नागरक	Nahgaraka	1.1
Nagareka paran	नगारे का परन	Nagahre kah paran	1.6.13
Nakhi	नखी	Nakhi	2.130
Nali	नली	Nalee	2.117
Namaskarki tihai	नमस्कारकी तिहाई	Namaskahrkee tihah-ee	1.6.15
Nara	नर	Nara	2.79, 3.6
Natikrisha	नातिकृश	Nahtikrusha	2.111
Natisthool	नातिस्थूल	Natisthoola	2.111
Nauhar	नौहार	Nauhahr	2.8
Nayaka	नायक	Nahyak	1.3.14
Nayak-nayika	नायक–नायिका	Nahyak nahyikah	2.98
Nibaddha	निबद्ध	Nibaddha	2.33, 2.80
Nibaddha tambura	निबद्ध तंबूरा	Nibaddha tamboorah	3.13

Nikas	निकास	Nikahs	2.81
Nikharaja	निखरजा	Nikhrajah	2.82
Nimish	निमिष	Nimish	2.83
Nirgeet	निर्गीत	Nirgeet	2.84, 2.141
Nishabda	नि:शब्द	Nishabda	2.86
Nishad	निषाद	Nishahd	2.108
Nishkala	निष्कल	Nishkala	2.85
Nissar	नि:सार	Nihsaar	2.110
Nom-tom	नोम्-तोम्	Nomtom	1.5.10, 2.8
Nrityangi paran	नृत्यांगी परन	Nrutyah(n)gee paran	1.6.13
Nrittyanuga	नृत्यानुग	Nrutyahnuga	Preface, 3
Nyasa	न्यास	Nyahsa	2.87

'O'

Odava	ओडव	Od(d)ava	2.96, 2.126
Ogha	ओघ	Ogha	2.141

'P'

Pada	पद	Pada	1.5.3, 2.88
Padar	पडार	Pad(d)ahr	1.6.12
Padashrit	पदाश्रित	Padahshrit	1.5.11
Padhant	पढंत	Pad(d)hanta	2.89
Padya	पद्य	Padya	2.88
Pakad	पकड	Pakad(d)	2.90
Pakhawaj	पखावज	Pakhahvaj	3.8
Pakshavadya	पक्षवाद्य	Pakshavahdya	3.8
Pala	पाला	Pahlah	3.12
Palta	पलटा	Palt(t)ah	1.6.15
Palti	पलटी	Palt(t)ee	2.126
Palavapada	पालवपद	Pahlavapada	2.30
Panchama	पंचम	Panchama	2.108
Pandit	पंडित	Pand(d)it	1.3.15

Proudha	प्रौढ	Praud(d)ha	2.111
Pudi	पुडी	Pud(d)ee	2.14
Pukar	पुकार	Pukahr	2.94
Punjab ang	पंजाब अंग	Punjahb ang	2.95
Punjabi	पंजाबी	Panjahbee	1.5.28
Pushkar	पुष्कर	Pushkar	3.8
Pushkarvadya	पुष्करवाद्य	Pushkarvahdya	3.8
Pushta	पुष्ट	Pusht(t)a	2.78

'Q'

Qaid	कैद	Kaid	2.8
Qawwal	कव्वाल	Kavvahl	1.3.17
Qawwal bacche	कव्वाल बच्चे	Kavvahl bachhe	1.5.18
Qawwali	कव्वाली	Kavvahlee	1.5.18
Qayada	कायदा	Kahyda	1.6.15

'R'

Rabab	रबाब	Rabahb	3.11
Radif	रदीफ़	Radeef	1.5.12
Raga	राग	Rahga	2.96
Raktibhava	रक्तिभव	Raktibhava	2.111
Raga-ragini	राग-रागिणी	Rahga rahgin(n)ee	2.98
Raganga- **paddhati**	रागांग-पद्धति	Rahgah(n)ga paddhati	2.97
Putra-vadhu	पुत्र-वधु	Putra vadhu	2.97
Ranjak	रंजक	Ranjak	1.3.7
Ras	रास	Rahs	1.5.24
Ras ka paran	रास का परन	Rahs kah paran	1.6.13
Rasika	रसिक	Rasika	1.3.7
Rassi	रस्सी	Rassee	2.14
Rava	रव	Rava	2.78
Razakhani gat	रझाखानी गत	Razahkhahnee gat	1.6.4

'S'

Sangatiya	संगतिया	Sangatiyah	1.4.4
Sangeet	संगीत	Sangeet	2.104
Sangeet-lekhana	संगीत लेखन	Sangeet lekhan	2.105
Sangeet-shastra	संगीत शास्त्र	Sangeet shastra	2.106
Sankirna	संकीर्ण	Sankeern(n)a	2.61, 2.96
Sansthana	संस्थान	Sansthahna	2.71, 2.107, 2.135
Santir	संतिर	Santir	3.9
Santoor	संतूर	Santoor	3.9
Saptak	सप्तक	Saptaka	2.108
Sarabat	सरबाट	Sarabaht(t)	3.11
Sarada-vina	शारदा-वीणा	Shardah veen(n)ah	3.11
Saral	सरल	Saral	2.96
Sarang	सारंग	Sahrang	3.10
Saranga	सारंगा	Sahrangah	3.10
Sarangi	सारंगी	Sahrangee	3.10
Sarang-vina	सारंग वीणा	Sahrang veen(n)ah	3.10
Saraswati-vina	सरस्वती वीणा	Sarasvati vee(n)nah	3.3
Sargam	सरगम	Sargam	1.5.20
Sargam geet	सरगम गीत	Sargamgeet	1.5.20
Sarika	सारिका	Sahrika	2.130
Sarod	सरोद	Sarod	3.11
Sarode	सरोद	Sarod	3.11
Sarthak paran	सार्थक परन	Sahrthak paran	1.6.13
Sashabda	सशब्द	Sashabda	2.86
Sath	साथ	Sahth	1.4.5, 1.6.17, 2.8
Sath paran	साथ परन	Sahth paran	1.6.13
Sawan	सावन	Sahvan	1.5.21
Sawan-hindola	सावन-हिंडोला	Sahvan hind(d)olah	1.5.21
Sayamgeya	सायंगेय	Sahya(n)geya	2.96
Saz	साझ	Sahz	1.4.2
Sazinda	साजिंदा	Sahjindah	1.4.2
Seedhi gat	सीधी गत	Seedhee gat	1.6.4
Seedhi tihai	सीधी तिहाई	Seedhee tihaee	1.6.4

Skandha pattika	स्कंध पट्रिका	Skandha pat(t)t(t)ikah	2.14
Snigdha	स्निग्ध	Snigdha	2.111
Soma	सोम	Soma	1.3.6
Sparsh	स्पर्श	Sparsha	2.113
Sphutita	स्फुटित	Sphut(t)ita	2.110
Srota	स्रोत	Srota	2.125
Srotogata	स्रोतोगता	Srotogatah	2.125
Sruti	श्रुति	Shruti	2.115
Sthana	स्थान	Sthahna	2.114
Sthayi	स्थायी	Sthahyee	1.5.10, 2.7, 2.147
Sukhavaha	सुखावह	Sukhahva-ha	2.111
Sukshma	सूक्ष्म	Sookshma	2.78, 2.120
Sumiran	सुमिरन	Sumiran	1.5.14
Sunadi	सुनाडि	Sunahd(d)i	3.12
Sundar singar paran	सुंदर सिंगार परन	Sundar singahr paran	1.6.13
Sundri	सुंद्री	Sundree	3.12
Sur	सुर	Sur	1.4.6, 2.116, 3.6
Suravarta	सुरावर्त	Surahvarta	1.6.18
Surbahar	सुरबहार	Surba-hahr	3.14
Sur bharana	सूर भरना	Soor bharnah	1.4.6
Sur dena	सूर देना	Soor dena	1.4.6
Surnai	सुरनई	Surnaee	3.12
Sushira	सुषिर	Sushira	2.117, 2.144
Swana	स्वन	Swana	2.78
Swara	स्वर	Swara	2.118
Swaradhun	स्वरधुन	Swaradhun	1.6.3
Swaradnyana	स्वरज्ञान	Swaradnyahna	2.120
Swaralekhana	स्वरलेखन	Swaralekhana	2.105
Swaralipi	स्वरलिपी	Swaralipee	2.119
Swarantara	स्वरांतर	Swarahntara	2.126
Swararth	स्वरार्थ	Swarahrtha	1.5.20
Swarasanchalana	स्वरसंचालन	Swarasanchahlana	2.121
Swarashrit	स्वराश्रित	Swarahshrit	1.5.11

'T'

Taraf	तरफ	Taraf	2.130
Tarana	तराना	Tarahnah	1.5.22
Taranga-vadya	तरंगवाद्य	Taranga vahdya	2.128
Tar-shehnai	तार शहनाई	Tahr sha-hanah-ee	3.17
Tarata	तारता	Tahrtah	2.129
Tarz	तर्ज	Tarz	2.23
Tasheka paran	ताशोका परन	Tahshekah paran	1.6.13
Tata	तत	Tata	2.130, 2.144
Tatanaddha	ततानद्ध	Tatahnaddha	2.131
Teep	टीप	T(t)eep	2.132
Teepa	टीपा	T(t)eepah	2.132
Tehttis dha paran	तेहत्तीस धा परन	Tehattees dhah paran	1.6.13
Tek	टेक	T(t)ek	1.5.3
Tenak	तेनक	Tenak	2.133
Tena-shabda	तेन शब्द	Ten shabda 1.5.10 1.5.10, 1.5.22	
Thap	थाप	Thahp	2.134
Thapiya Baj	थपिया बाज	Thahpiyah bahj	2.134
That	थाट	Thaht(t)	2.71, 2.135
Thath	ठाठ	T(t)haht(t)h	2.125
Theka	ठेका	T(t)hekah	1.6.20, 2.125
Thok	ठोक	T(t)hok	2.8/
Thumri	ठुमरी	T(t)humri	1.5.28
Tihai	तिहाई	Tihah-ee	1.6.15, 1.6.21
Tihai gat	तिहाई गत	Tihah-ee gat	1.6.44
Tipalli gat	तिपल्ली गत	Tipalli gat	1.6.4
Tipperi	टिप्पेरी	T(t)ipperee	3.1
Tirip	तिरिप	Tirip	2.32
Tisra	तिस्र	Tisra	2.61, 2.125
Titodi paran	टिटोडी परन	T(t)it(t)od(d)ee paran	1.6.13
Tivrata	तीव्रता	Teevratah	2.136
Toda	तोडा	Tod(d)ah	1.6.22
Topki paran	तोपकी परन	Topkee paran	1.6.13
Tribhina	त्रिभिन्न	Tribhinna	2.32
Trikon	त्रिकोन	Trikon	2.130
Tripadi	त्रिपदी	Tripadee	1.5.28

Vaggeyakara	वाग्गेयकार	Vahggeyakahra	1.5.11, 2.145
Vak	वाक्	Vahk	2.145
Vakra	वक्र	Vakra	2.96
Vamshi	वंशी	Va(n)shee	3.1
Vama	वाम	Vahma	3.15
Vana	वाण	Vahn(n)a	3.9
Varjya	वर्ज्य	Varjya	2.146
Varjita	वर्जित	Varjita	2.146
Varna	वर्ण	Varn(n)a	2.147
Varnalankara	वर्णलिंकार	Varn(n)ah-lankahra	2.7
Vartika	वार्तिक	Vahtrika	2.151
Vasant panchami	वसंत पंचमी	Vasant panchami	1.1.9
Venu	वेणु	Ven(n)u	3.1
Vicchinna	विच्छिन्न	Vichchinna	2.70
Vichitra been	विचित्र बीन	Vichitra been	3.2
Vidara	विदार	Vidahra	2.148
Vikrut	विकृत	Vikrut	2.96
Vilambita	विलंबित	Vilambita	2.60
Viloma	विलोम	Viloma	2.149
Vinyasa	विन्यास	Vinyasa	2.87
Violin	वॉयलिन	Violin	3.18
Vina	वीणा	Veen(n)ah	3.3
Vishamahata	विषमाहत	Vishamah-hata	2.70
Vishnupada	विष्णुपद	Vishn(n)upadi	1.5.29
Vistara	विस्तार	Vistahra	1.3.15, 2.8.2.150
Vitata	वितत	Vitata	2.131
Vivadi	विवादी	Vivahdee	2.142
Vritti	वृत्ति	Vrutti	2.151
Vyavasaya	व्यवसाय	Vyavasahya	1.3.20
Vyavasayika	व्यावसायिक	Vyavasahyika	1.3.20

'Y'

Yati	यति	Yati	2.125